"Cooper, do yo
chance of getting out alive?"

Mack Bolan eyed the wiry fighter. "A mission is a fifty-fifty proposition. Lady Luck can screw up any plan. If you think I've been feeding you a line, then you know where the door is."

"You'd go a man short?" Basayev asked.

"Better five men at one hundred percent than six when you're carrying one who isn't."

The Chechen shrugged. "Okay. For the money, I'm in."

As Grimaldi lifted the chopper into the air, the Executioner settled into his seat, wondering if having to settle for the men he could get at such short notice would result in more problems than he could handle.

They were a motley crew, and this was going to be more of a difficult mission than he had envisioned.

MACK BOLAN ®
The Executioner

The Executioner®
Don Pendleton's

REBEL BLAST

A GOLD EAGLE BOOK FROM
W✺RLDWIDE®

TORONTO • NEW YORK • LONDON
AMSTERDAM • PARIS • SYDNEY • HAMBURG
STOCKHOLM • ATHENS • TOKYO • MILAN
MADRID • WARSAW • BUDAPEST • AUCKLAND

Recycling programs
for this product may
not exist in your area.

First edition November 2013

ISBN-13: 978-0-373-64420-9

Special thanks and acknowledgment to
Andy Boot for his contribution to this work.

REBEL BLAST

Neither dead nor alive, the hostage is suspended by an incalculable outcome. It is not his destiny that awaits him, nor his own death, but anonymous chance, which can only seem to him something absolutely arbitrary.... He is in a state of radical emergency, of virtual extermination.
—Jean Baudrillard,
1929–2007

The U.S. may not negotiate with terrorists, but she will never abandon hostages, leave her citizens in harm's way. In their darkest hour, they will have a champion.
—Mack Bolan

THE
MACK BOLAN
LEGEND

Nothing less than a war could have fashioned the destiny of the man called Mack Bolan. Bolan earned the Executioner title in the jungle hell of Vietnam.

But this soldier also wore another name—Sergeant Mercy. He was so tagged because of the compassion he showed to wounded comrades-in-arms and Vietnamese civilians.

Mack Bolan's second tour of duty ended prematurely when he was given emergency leave to return home and bury his family, victims of the Mob. Then he declared a one-man war against the Mafia.

He confronted the Families head-on from coast to coast, and soon a hope of victory began to appear. But Bolan had broken society's every rule. That same society started gunning for this elusive warrior—to no avail.

So Bolan was offered amnesty to work within the system against terrorism. This time, as an employee of Uncle Sam, Bolan became Colonel John Phoenix. With a command center at Stony Man Farm in Virginia, he and his new allies—Able Team and Phoenix Force—waged relentless war on a new adversary: the KGB.

But when his one true love, April Rose, died at the hands of the Soviet terror machine, Bolan severed all ties with Establishment authority.

Now, after a lengthy lone-wolf struggle and much soul-searching, the Executioner has agreed to enter an "arm's-length" alliance with his government once more, reserving the right to pursue personal missions in his Everlasting War.

1

Viktor Adamenko remembered that time. Not well, but rather with the imprecise and impressionistic memory of the young. If he closed his eyes, it flooded back to him in a tidal wave of sound, sight and smell that threatened to engulf him. He had once read of a French writer for whom the taste of a small cake could conjure up a lifetime of experience. Adamenko felt much the same, though he thought it effete to be so influenced by a cake. Still, that was the French for you. Only a man schooled in a world where life was cheap and yet the striving to prolong it so expensive could appreciate that there were elements that were far more evocative.

For Adamenko it was the smell of tear gas. CS, perhaps, or any other chemical formula designed to have the same effect. Only the slightest aroma in the nose, tickling at the back of the throat and bringing forth that almost exquisite rawness that presaged the tears and the pain: that was all it would take to transport him back to that time, when he had been young. That time when he had discovered, with the kind of jolt that would make a lesser man bleat to his superiors about counseling and stress, that life was tenuous and random, likely to be snatched away on nothing more than whim or error.

Sometimes, in the middle of an attack situation, he

would delay slipping on his gas mask for the briefest of seconds, wanting to catch just the faintest wisp of CS on the breeze before common sense prevailed. It was not just the memory and all that it meant: it was the result it had on him.

The Vikings had Beserkers, men driven into a bloodlust fury where they were nothing more than killing machines. The Chechen National Socialist group had Adamenko. When the memories came back to him, they triggered within him the rage of impotence that he had felt at that time. The guilt, anger and fury that he had kept barely contained within him for the intervening years, and for which he now found release in his commitment to the cause.

Adamenko was a useful tool. He was a weapon that could be used with the certain knowledge that the only thing to stop him would be his own death.

He never said why this happened when the CS was in the air. No one knew of his past; he never spoke of it. There may have been some who had guessed, but they were wise enough to keep their own counsel. Adamenko was not a man who encouraged idle chatter or conversation of a personal nature. He was a bear of a man, and amiable in his own way, but not someone who could be engaged on any level other than the superficial or the abstract. There was something about his demeanor that warned against trying.

But the man remembered, the intermittent memory of the child who could not assimilate the events around him. The intermittent memory of the child who had been injured, whose brain had been partially damaged by wounding and more: the memory of the child who had lost his parents and had spent his early teenage years in orphanages, fighting off the abuse of those fellow inmates who found him slow, and the more sinister abuse of those staff who sought to take advantage of that very slowness. This was the intermittent memory of the man who had so much that he wanted to block out, and yet was compelled by his own psyche to remember some of the most painful parts of that past.

It had been a visit to the theater, on a family trip to Moscow, a rare treat in a time when there was little money to fritter on luxuries. It had been only a few years since the Communists had crumbled, and even fewer since the Russians had finally complied with the request for the Chechen Republic to part company with the old patronage. Even so, it was still a time of change, and a time when things were in flux.

He could not remember what he had seen; only that he had been happy. This, he had come to realize over the years, was a fragile state that could so easily be snatched away by chance or design. As it had been that night: from the back of the hall, there had been a wave of confusion and panic, the noises of men shouting while others screamed. Turning in his seat, he could still feel the arms of his mother smother and engulf him as she sought to shelter him. He could remember seeing, from an obtuse angle as he twisted to free himself, the men coming down the aisles. Balaclavas hid their faces, and they were in black. Guns were leveled on the audience, sweeping over them in threatening arcs, and he could smell the sweat of fear as it seeped from the pores of those around him. There had been no gunfire at this stage, but the threat of it had been enough to keep people in their seats.

There had been a lull while the crowd, cowed from their initial panicked desire to rise and run, kept low and silent. In this space, came empty shouted words, the rhetoric of politics that he now knew so well. There was aim, there was action and there were words. The first two he had time for; the latter was a waste. It had been that night.

He had no sense of the time that had followed in that siege; he knew of the scale only because of what he had later learned. All he had were snapshots. There were the men among the hostages whose patience had frayed, and who had been the first to rise and shoot off their mouths. Shots of a different kind had greeted their dissent. This had, in its turn, led to more panic, which had been quickly quelled. He was only a child, but already Viktor Adamenko had learned one thing: even the men who held the guns, who held the whip hand, were just as liable to fear and indecision as those they sought to oppress.

There had been no word from the outside. Something about full succession and a fully constituted republic had been in the barrage of words that had been yelled. No Russians would tell them what to do at any level: that was all they meant, dressed up in big words and long phrases.

Viktor was still a child to these men: yet even then he could have told them that the words were meaningless unless they followed up with action. And what action was it to take hostage the very people you were supposedly freeing? Not everyone in the theater was Chechen, but the young Viktor supposed as much. What if there were other families like his present?

These men were fools. The Russians had bigger guns, they had tanks; he had seen them on television. The Russians did not like being ordered around by those who were smaller than them. The fall of the Soviet had been a massive blow to the pride of the Russia that had been at its hub, and any fool knew that they were looking for an excuse to show how strong and important they still could be.

The smell: fear, the stench of blood and flesh as it decayed, and the urine and feces as the toilets backed up and the hours stretched to days; the smell of sweat and fear as it stayed in the clothing, welling up as people tried to keep warm and feel secure by huddling together.

The smell, mostly, of the anesthetic gas that had been pumped into the theater. The confusion and dreamlike state that followed was like being on the edge of sleep and yet still awake enough to know what was happening around him.

And then confusion, pain and fear as the world seemed to cave in around them: the pounding of the artillery outside as the theater was shelled, the choking dust and falling masonry as the building was buffeted. The men who had seemed so assured and in charge but a short time before were torn between flight and attack—but their attack was focused only on those who were their hostages, and who were supposedly their own people. Again, this was an impression of the stupidity and hypocrisy of these people that had always stayed with Viktor and had colored the way he looked at his own allies.

Through the smoke there had been a charge: gas-masked Russians, yelling incomprehensibly and firing on anyone and anything that moved. His father was already dead, killed by a chunk of ceiling that had made mush of his head. Now his mother died, killed by the raking fire of Russian soldiers who made no distinction between the captors and the captives. They only wanted to assert their power. It was another lesson for him to learn and carry with him.

His life was saved only by his mother laying herself over him, giving up her own life so that he might live. She absorbed the gunfire so that he might live. Her body stopped the anesthetic being absorbed into his lungs as it had for so many: the many who had been killed not by the gunfire, but by the gas designed to make it safe for the Russians to enter. Her double sacrifice had saved his life. But for what?

His hatred of the Russians had grown over the years to the point where it had become a mania. This, again, made him useful to some.

Alexsandr Orlov was one such man, the self-appointed leader and strategist of the Chechen National Socialists, and a man who had his own demons. He recognized in Adamenko those qualities that made for a terrorist: monomania—the desire to impose your view on others regardless of their own views, and an intolerance of anything that was not, in your view, right.

Orlov had met Adamenko in one of the many homes that he, too, had lived in as an orphan. He had been a victim of the Chechen revolution but in another way. His family had been in the path of a Russian detachment that had been patrolling the border area. The family farm had supplied them with what they'd needed: food, vodka and women. But this had been taken against the will of the family, and so there was evidence to clear away. Bullets and the cleansing power of fire had seen to it.

Orlov, on the hills when the Russians arrived, had stayed clear and then seen it happen, powerless to intervene. That was why he understood the guilt that drove his Beserker onward.

Between them, the two young men had emerged from the hell of their childhood and adolescence with the desire to distance themselves from the Russians they hated as a driving force. So it was that the current Chechen regime, forced by economic necessity to get into bed with those who had until so recently ruled over them, was an object of hatred. They were worse than the despised Russians because they colluded with them.

To be Chechen was a thing to aspire to: not least because

it meant that you were not Russian. In the same way, the group's ideals of extreme ethnic cleansing for the Chechen people was fueled less by the desire for racial purity per se than the need to expunge any taint of Russian blood from the land.

This clarity of purpose—the very thing that both young men believed every other political group lacked—was a driving and dangerous force.

As one town was soon to find out.

"THEY CALL THIS a hotel? The water is cold and the beer is warm," Todd Slaughter intoned as he twisted the hot faucet on the tub.

"That doesn't even make sense," Bryan Freeman said from the adjoining room. "If you're going to try to be Groucho, then at least learn the damn lines properly." He wandered into the bathroom, peering over the top of his spectacles, the monitor printouts still hanging from his right hand.

"Just trying to lighten the mood and not feel so frustrated at this third world state," Slaughter said as he let the tepid water run down the drain. "I suppose I don't have to take a bath. I could just stink like the food."

"Man, you've really got a downer on this place," Freeman said calmly. "Why don't you try my room? I haven't had any trouble with my plumbing."

"Lucky you," Slaughter replied sarcastically.

"Yeah, well, maybe you should try talking nicely to it. Actually, maybe you should try talking nicely to anyone or anything. If these tests prove to be correct, then this is not going to be a third world country for much longer."

"It isn't now. I was being unkind to the third world," Slaughter commented as he dried his hands, then took the printouts from his colleague. "What do they say?"

"They say that we haven't been wasting our time. The gas might have been a strike, but the mineral deposits are right where we figured."

"Does Lisa know what this says?" Slaughter asked.

Freeman grinned. "Not yet. If she did, then we'd already have half the engineering force down on us, ready to dig, before any contracts were in place."

Slaughter returned the smile. "Then maybe we should go and tell her. I'll hold her down and stop her from getting too excited."

Freeman agreed. Although they were only too happy to joke about it now, Lisa Acquero, their manager and expedition head, had been on their case all week, pushing for results. No matter how many times Freeman or Slaughter tried to explain to her that data could only be analyzed when tests were completed, and those tests were reliant on reactions that took time to be effected, all she could come back with was a litany of the pressure that she was under from the Chechen government, the U.S. State Department and the major mining companies whose consortium had used the financial and political muscle to set up this uneasy liaison.

"I'm only telling you this to bring home to you guys how much I'm taking the heat and keeping it off you," had become her constant refrain, seemingly blissfully free of any knowledge of the irony. Slaughter had been keen to point out to her how the transfer of pressure was affected by her attitude, but the calmer head of Freeman had stayed his hand.

"Now you have no need to hold me back," he said smugly as they approached her room.

"Hey, I wasn't doing it for you," Freeman remarked. "You think I want to be stuck here with you two at loggerheads?"

"Fair point, Bryan. Remind me to do the same for you sometime," Slaughter said as he entered Acquero's room without bothering to knock.

"Again, it would be nice if what you said made sense," Freeman muttered, shaking his head as he followed, knowing that Slaughter was not listening.

Inside her room, Acquero was pacing by the window, listening intently to her cell phone and only occasionally managing to get a word in by way of response. Her stiff posture told Freeman that just maybe she hadn't been feeding them a line all this time. He could almost feel sympathy for her as she struggled to put across what was happening.

"...Okay, that's true, but...These are trained engineers and analysts we have here. Of course a twelve-strong team costs money, but...You can't hurry that...but...no, it doesn't work like that. I'm assured that the tests...Of course you'll get the results as soon as I—"

Slaughter picked his moment. As she spoke, he thrust the printout under her nose. She stopped speaking as she looked at it. On the other end of the cell phone, Freeman could hear the barking of an executive unused to being ignored. Acquero looked at the figures, frowned and then looked at Slaughter.

"Does this mean what I think it does?" Slaughter nodded, and the woman momentarily returned her attention to the cell phone. "I'll call you back in ten. This is important." She killed the phone call, leaving the executive to fume impotently on another continent.

She took the printouts from the analyst and scanned them again. "Bear in mind I'm not an expert and it's been a long time since they last sent me to head up an operation like this. This looks like the mineral deposits under this region are bigger than we could have hoped for."

"That about sums it up. Of course, their positioning

makes it a little difficult to mine. The soil and rock strata in that area can be a little unstable, so it will cost a sizable outlay to tunnel safely."

She waved dismissively. "The government here will pay for that, long term. We pay them for a license to mine, then loan them the money to start mining. They contract us, and give us back our own money."

"Meanwhile, the license we have to pay them we recoup in consultancy fees for the pleasure of being here," Freeman added with a sardonic grin.

"Pleasure?" Slaughter queried with a moue of distaste as he eyed the Chechen idea of a luxury suite.

"Dude, with the money they're going to make from this even after the company takes its cut, they'll be able to build a palace to rival Vegas," Freeman told him.

"The company will leave them with that much?" Slaughter queried.

"We are very fair with our partnering states and governments," Acquero interjected, mindful that the room may be bugged and that these men were employees under her charge and should at least keep their views to themselves.

"Lisa, you kept a straight face," Freeman quipped. "Hey, they pay us. We have no right to take the moral high ground when we take the money. Besides, now that we've got the results, things will start moving back home, right?"

"Contractual discussions will commence, of course," Acquero began, "but in the interim we may be asked to stay on and act as consultants for the Chechen government as they have no experience of such delicate matters."

"Of course," Freeman said dryly. "So I guess we don't get to go home yet?"

"That depends on head office and what its decision is," she began, hitting speed dial on her cell phone. "It'll be twenty-four hours before we get a decision, so in the meantime I suggest you take the chance to chill out a little."

"Yeah, there's so much we can do," Slaughter murmured. Then his face creased in a frown and he moved closer to the window, peering past his boss. She looked at him askance as her phone was answered on the other side of the world.

"I haven't seen any marked vehicles like those," Slaughter stated as he indicated two trucks and four military-style jeeps on the street below. "I wonder what—"

In an office in New York, those were the only words heard from Lisa Acquero's cell phone before the line went dead.

It was thirty seconds before the executive staring at his phone snapped out of his trance and dialed a Washington number.

2

"You know, of course, that it was known for some time as the Mineral Republic, and although there was proof of this, under the Soviet regime it was always hard for us to gauge the truth of how much, and how much work mining these minerals had been undertaken."

"Even with our intelligence services—or yours, come to that?"

There was silence at the other end of the phone. Hal Brognola could envisage the executive smiling softly before answering in his blandest tone. "Of course, Hal, I have no idea what you mean by that. We are a commercial company, and as such we have alliances with other companies who have similar interests. There is some sharing of information for business needs, but beyond that—"

The big Fed shook his head and chewed his lip, biting back the comments that immediately sprung to mind. Instead he said, "Of course, Mr. Billings. What was I thinking? Our government departments would, in the same way, never divulge more than was necessary." He added to himself, Unless the kickback had been large enough or it suited whichever cabal within the services had the relevant agenda.

"I'm glad we're on the same page, Hal," Billings continued. "Since the second war in the region, we have sought to forge links that could be of benefit to all parties."

The big Fed gritted his teeth. The hope that his emphasis on referring to the man by title would be taken up had either been ignored or unnoticed. Brognola was a fair man. Perhaps this executive made a habit of referring to those he spoke to but had no prior relationship with in an informal manner to put them at ease. Perhaps. To Brognola, it just sounded patronizing and as though the man assumed he had command over the government officer he was speaking to. It wasn't something that endeared him to the man he was speaking with.

"I'm assuming that when you speak of all parties, you're referring to the Russians, as well," Brognola said softly. The pause at the end of the line told him all he needed to know. He went on. "So would I be correct, then, in assuming that this is a little more of a local arrangement?"

"At this stage, seeing as the mission was more by way of expedition than anything else, it was decided that the Chechen Assembly would work directly with us, and the Russian authorities would be informed should it deem necessary to move larger numbers of men and equipment into the region. Of course, they would be delighted to welcome trade and industry to a region that has struggled economically for the past quarter century."

"Delighted" was not the word Brognola would have chosen. The Russian president was combative at the best of times, and with mineral rights for the region sewn up between a U.S.-based mining cartel and a regional authority that was in a relationship both implicit and explicit with the Russian overlords, he would be less than pleased that his government got a third-hand, reduced share in the spoils.

For a moment Brognola wondered if he should try to explain the complex nature of the political relationships in the North Caucasus to Billings, but then decided either that the man had full knowledge and had been deputed to make a move that took that into account, or that he had no idea and didn't care. Either way, it wasn't worth Brognola wasting his breath.

Instead he said, "Really. It sounds like a winner all 'round, Mr. Billings. Which leads me to two questions. One, in that case, what does it have to do with me? And two, how did you get access to this number?"

ARGUN-MARTAN STOOD ON the bank of the Terek, at a point on the river where a twisting bend took it around the base of a mountain. The shallow cove made by the bend allowed the town to be secluded and relatively peaceful. That, and its proximity to the main mineral-bearing area as defined by initial surveys, made it a perfect location for the expeditionary mining party. By the same token, it also made it a perfect target for any group seeking to isolate and take over a town for its own ends.

It was unfortunate for the inhabitants of Argun-Martan—and the American party—that the very thing that made the town such a perfect base should also be the very thing that ensured its own capture.

Alexsandr Orlov could not believe his luck when the intelligence report first reached him. To make his group known on a international stage, to bring attention to its cause and also to ensure that his people were in a geographic position that would deter immediate Russian retaliation, he had picked this town after careful consideration. It had a small population, a lazy and corrupt police force even by Russian standards, which would capitulate quickly rather than risk its own deaths, and only one real route in and out, which would make it easy to secure for a group that was long on determination but short on human resources.

For that town to then become a place where foreign nationals were present, well, that was more than an invitation, it was a gift. The fact that they were involved in mining and surveying meant little if nothing to Orlov. To grow up as an orphan in a land where your heritage had been raped by successive governments and occupying forces meant that the notion that the land had any intrinsic worth was an alien concept. Orlov saw only that these foreigners represented both a way to get more worldwide publicity for his cause, and also a way in which more money may be squeezed from their homeland for their return.

Timing was everything in life. It was poor timing for the survey and expedition party to have not left town a day before; poor for them to suddenly come into information that multiplied their worth and made them all the more valuable to secure as hostages. It was good timing for Orlov and his group that they'd chosen this day to mount their invasion, seeing as they caught the foreigners at the peak of their earning power. On the other hand, if Orlov could have seen into the future, he may have seen it as a very poor piece of timing. In truth, he may have been better off abandoning his plans: not that it seemed that way when he stood in his jeep and announced that the Chechen National Socialists had now assumed control of Argun-Martan.

"I DO NOT like the look of this at all," Bryan Freeman breathed. In the pit of his stomach, a low growl signaled that his irritable bowel was echoing his thoughts. Freeman was a great believer in instinct. Flight or fight was a trigger to his condition, and he knew what he should be doing right now. Instead he stood rooted to the spot at Lisa Acquero's shoulder, while Todd Slaughter spoke what, in

Freeman's opinion, was the biggest crock he had heard in a long time.

"Man, if this is all they can muster for military maneuvers, then God help them if the Russians decide to clamp down."

"Fool—the Russians are the military around here," Acquero replied. "No, this must be some kind of local militia. Civil defense, I guess."

Scratch that previous thought. Slaughter had come out with the second biggest crock. This little beauty won by a mile. When he spoke, Freeman had trouble keeping his voice even.

"Far be it from me to burst any bubble of inane theorizing you might have, people, but can I point out two things. First, if there was any kind of militia or military action planned for around here, then the mayor or whatever the fuck he's called around here would have told you about it, Lisa. Second, if they were Russians, Todd, they would have insignia and uniforms and not be dressed like they were the fucking Taliban. Jesus, don't you ever watch CNN? Actually, there's a third thing… Look at that. You think any kind of planned action is going to make the locals act like that?"

Acquero and Slaughter followed Freeman's pointing index finger. It was trembling, more from fear than indignation. Down in the street below them, the convoy of vehicles had come to a halt as two police cars screeched to halt, turning across the width of the street to try to block it, their sirens wailing briefly before they were silenced.

Even though the window was closed, they were still close enough to hear the exchanges in the street below. None of them could claim to have a fluency in either Russian or the local dialect, having relied on interpreters for much of their stay, but Freeman had a smattering of the dialect picked up through a good ear for languages. As he roughly translated for Slaughter and Acquero, he began to think that ignorance would have been bliss.

"Ah—the cop is yelling something like 'what the fuck do you think you're doing and who are you?' Aw, man, that's not going to go down well—"

"What isn't?" Acquero asked.

"The asshole just asked the guy standing in the jeep if he was the son of a whore with syphilis and if this had softened his brain. Man, that's stupid when you're outnumbered like that."

"I don't know, maybe it's just a show of bravado," Slaughter muttered.

Freeman looked at the engineer as though he were an idiot, and then returned his attention to the scene below them.

"My cell phone went down when they came up. You think they're running some kind of interference?" Acquero asked, staring blankly at the phone as it began to dawn on her that their situation was less than promising.

"If they're the bad guys, then they've killed the tower, hon," Freeman said softly. Reception was poor in this region, and they relied on one satellite link relay mast that was five miles outside the town, placed in the only spot for some distance that was live. That would make perfect sense. He wasn't exactly sure what they wanted, but Freeman definitely had them tagged as the bad guys. And it looked as though he was about to find out just how bad...

The guy standing in the jeep exited the vehicle and stepped onto the road. He was of average height and skinny. His mode of dress looked odd, but there was something about his bearing that screamed he was the leader. It also screamed that he was dangerous: not that the opposing police chief seemed to notice that.

Used to having his own way, the police chief left his men—five armed men who looked as if they wanted to be anywhere else, and had a clearer grasp of the danger than their boss—and started to swagger toward the lead truck. The driver sat impassive, whoever or whatever was in the covered rear staying, for the moment, under wraps.

Freeman did a quick calculation in his head. This was not a large town, and as they had been resident for a month, come Friday, he was pretty sure that he had a measure of how big the police force was. By his reckoning, there was only double the number of men now on the street. Maybe half a dozen at most. Looking at the jeeps and the trucks, he could count more men than that in the convoy, regardless of whether there were any hidden in the covered backs of the trucks.

The police chief was either incredibly brave or incredibly stupid. It was only conscience and judgment that made the line between.

As the police chief reached the front of the lead truck, the other man held up a hand to stop him. Either because the man exuded authority, or just because he was baffled, the police chief halted for a moment.

"Viktor, the local law corruption needs persuading of our credentials," Freeman heard the man say in a calm voice that was not raised yet still managed to carry across the eerily silent street.

The convoy had come to rest in such a manner that the trucks—to point and rear of the jeeps—were on the right hand side of the road while the jeeps were over to the left. That had enabled the man to make immediate eye contact with the police as they'd blocked the road, and had presumably been a part of his plan. In his mind's eye, things were going exactly as he'd envisaged them.

The flap at the rear of the lead truck moved slightly and,

with a grace and speed that belied his height and bulk, a man alighted and moved around so that he was facing the hesitant police chief.

Freeman, watching from the window, wanted to yell at the law officer to turn and run. He had the chance. The giant of a man turned and grunted, assenting gently to some unspoken order from his commander.

The police chief fell into the incredibly stupid camp. There was no doubt about this in the American's mind as he watched him stand, rigid in fear, while the man called Viktor approached him. He was calm, moving in measured strides that ate up the ground and spoke of his height. He was bareheaded, with cropped hair and a small goatee beard to match. Whereas the other men in the convoy were dressed in Islamic hill dress, Viktor looked like the soldier he either was, or had been at some time. He was tall—maybe six two or three—but there was something about his bearing that made him look taller still.

Freeman had a really bad feeling about this as the soldier stopped in front of the police chief and stared him down. The chief quailed visibly, and Freeman noted with a chill feeling that the other man seemed to smile as he watched this unfold.

"This is our town now," he said simply. "Your men will surrender their arms to us. I want all town officials to meet with me at the municipal building in thirty minutes. I will give you that long to round them up. It will be useless for them to try and run. You will also find that their will be no communication with either Grozny or Moscow. We have temporarily disabled the telephone and cell phone relays, and they will be reinstituted only when I am satisfied that we are in agreement. Do I make myself perfectly clear?"

The police chief looked at him as though he were insane. Freeman figured that he probably was, as there was something chilling in his matter-of-fact tone.

"No. If I do that, then I will be stripped of my post. If that happens, I lose everything I have worked for." The police chief started to turn to walk away. "You are the fools. You think the president will like this when he hears about it, any more than he liked the theater?"

The words had an immediate effect on the giant called Viktor. The other man grinned happily. The police chief had no idea of the anger that his comment—designed to strike fear or apprehension—had generated in the man. At the very least, it could be described as the reverse of his intent.

At most, it was his death warrant.

Freeman had no more words to translate for his companions. The sight that unfolded below was conducted without speech and needed no explanation. As the police chief turned back to face the way he was walking, he did not see the giant take one last step so that he was on his prey.

That was the only word fitting enough. The older, smaller man was like a rodent swooped on by a bird of prey. Viktor's hands closed around the police chief's neck, pulling him backward and choking the breath from him so that he could not cry out. As he fell backward, the giant switched his grip with expert ease, so that the police chief pivoted as he fell, going down onto his knees and landing between the spread legs of the giant solider.

With a cold efficiency that was as chilling to watch, he calmly took the man's head in his hands, pinioned the police chief's body between his own knees and twisted once, with a violent jerk.

There was no scream, as Freeman would have expected, only the sickening crack of bone breaking. Viktor stepped back and let the body fall, turning away to face the remaining police before the corpse hit the road.

The police of Argun-Martan dropped their weapons, terrified. The man standing beside his jeep nodded with satisfaction.

In the hotel room, Slaughter turned away to vomit while Freeman felt cold sweat trickle down his spine. Acquero spoke for them all when she said, "Guys, I don't think the company will be able to negotiate or bribe us out of this."

3

"Who the hell is Billings? Why does he have my number? And what the hell does he—or you—expect me to do about what's going on? It would, for instance, help if I actually knew what was happening. Which I don't," Brognola added as an afterthought.

"Those are good questions, Hal, and they deserve an answer. But first I need an answer from you—why did you contact me?"

Brognola smiled, though it was almost entirely without humor. He was seated in a coffee shop on the edge of the Mall, a short distance from his office and from the office of the congressman who sat in front of him.

Declan MacManus was older than Brognola and heavier set. Whereas the big Fed still packed muscle, despite his years away from active service, the congressman was running to fat. The apple Danish with his latte wouldn't help. Brognola had espresso. He had hoped it would send some subliminal message to get the hell on with business. So far, it hadn't worked.

"Dec, you have a long history of lobbying with the mining industry, particularly those companies with strong overseas presence. You're an advocate of fossil and mineral fuels, and the finding of untapped reserves. You've also known me for a long time, and it would be kind of obvious for you to mention my name if there was a shit-storm on the horizon."

The congressman shrugged. "It doesn't mean I would actually do that, Hal."

"The hell it doesn't. Billings tossed your name around like it was supposed to make me roll over and beg."

"Ah...you have me dead to rights, then."

Brognola sighed. "You know, Dec, if there wasn't anything slightly off-kilter about what's going on with you and the industry, you wouldn't have wanted to meet me out of office, with no ears or eyes, although there could always be questions if we were seen together."

"Easily dismissed," the congressman said, shrugging. "We've known each other long enough for it to be a personal catch-up."

"Sure... Now how about we cut the crap?"

MacManus laughed shortly. "I knew Billings was some kind of lily-livered ass-wipe who would panic before he ascertained the full facts."

"Which are?" Brognola prompted.

"The simple fact is that we don't know yet. It's too early to make anything other than a guess."

"That doesn't answer why he had my number in the first place. You know Justice doesn't deal with diplomatic paths. That's State."

"You're right, of course," the congressman conceded. "There was always a chance that something could go wrong, and if it did then the usual paths may have been long-winded and ultimately useless. Which is why Billings had your number. I know you have the President's ear and can get things done. But I must stress that your number was only to be used as a last resort. It isn't that far down the line yet, which is why I'm pissed at him."

"I can't say I'm happy at either of you," Brognola stated.

"You should tell me about it. If it comes to the point where the President needs to be informed…"

The congressman blew out his cheeks, then frowned. "Look, it might be something and nothing, Hal. About eighteen months ago, a consortium of some of the largest mining and engineering corporations in the U.S.A. got wind of a report that came from an ex-Soviet mining engineer who had left the Ukraine and now worked here. He's nearing retirement, and happened to mention that one of the last things we worked on before the wall came down was an expedition in the North Caucasus, where the Chechen Republic now lies.

"This report revealed the potential for vast, untapped mineral fields. Back then, the Soviets didn't have the technology to mine in what was basically unstable ground, and so even though the area is known for its mineral reserves, this little baby got left. And, once the wall was down and all the ex-Soviet states were busy squabbling among themselves, it got forgotten…filed… Something…"

"Until your man mentioned it." Brognola nodded. "Did he have details?"

"After twenty or so years he couldn't remember too much, but the basics were enough to excite a lot of important people. He was given a stipend to reconstruct as much as possible, and then hand it over to his employers for a nice little bonus on retirement, which he did."

"The good company man. I guess that was instilled in him before Glasnost," Brognola stated. "So let me guess. A consortium was formed that could maneuver an expedition to Chechnya on some kind of pretext that wouldn't make the supposedly hands-off Russians suspicious—"

"Russia's president is hardly the world's most hands-off guy," the congressman interjected.

"There's understatement and absurdity," Brognola said.

"Anyway, your—sorry—this consortium's expedition had just turned up something of interest and were telling Billings all about it when they were cut off almost midsentence, like he was telling me."

"That's about the size of it. We don't know what's happened out there. It might just have been communications coming down, I mean, it's not an easy area to keep in the loop."

"But it might be more?"

"How can I honestly say? Yes, the Russians might have found out about the minerals. They'd have to be several shades of stupid to be so heavy-handed."

"Or just impetuous," Brognola mused. "There is one other thing that you haven't mentioned, or seem to have forgotten…" He watched the congressman's puzzled frown, then continued. "It doesn't have to be the Russians. They might control the State, but it's at a distance. Only five percent of the population is Russian. Ninety percent are Chechen. Sunni Muslims for the most part, and not enamored of the Russian way of living, or the Russian way of doing things. If it was the Russians, then there would have to be deployments. We would probably know about that. I've heard nothing, but I could double-check with a contact."

"That would set our—Billings's—mind at rest," the congressman commented. "You've been looking things up, Hal. Those are impressive statistics."

"Not if you just check Wikipedia." The big Fed smiled. "Something you should have done. Definitely something Billings should have done. Then you might have found out something else that should have set alarm bells ringing."

"Just because it's on Wiki doesn't mean it's true," the congressman said with a shrug.

Brognola shook his head. "No, this one I had personal

experience of back in the day. You'll have to take my word
on that. There was a time when the major economic force
in Chechnya was the generation of ransom money. Kidnapping wasn't just a national sport, it was the core industry. There was nothing else, and they were desperate
times. The first and second Chechen wars changed that.
But maybe not entirely…old habits can die hard, and if
there was the suspicion that your party and what they found
was worth serious money…"

"So what do we do?"

"Wait to see if there's a ransom demand. Meantime, let
me see what I can turn up. The way I see it, whatever's
going on out there, the possibility of using regular diplomatic channels is a slim chance to begin with. With what
I know about the region and its history, I'd say that your
man Billings may have panicked, but his gut reaction may
actually have been leading him in the right direction."

THE MINING AND engineering groups gathered in Slaughter's
suite—if the largish room with en suite facilities could be
termed such—after Freeman suggested to the still-shocked
Acquero that they gather everyone together. She looked at
him and asked why. For the life of him he had no real answer. What could they do under the circumstances? But
somehow it seemed that having everyone together would
give them some kind of strength in unity, whether it is for
morale or simply because they would be harder to separate
without each knowing what was happening to the other.

This was the largest hotel in town. It had been picked
for that reason, so that the groups could be under the same
roof and thus continue working at any hour of the day and
night. The fact that it was also the most luxurious accom-
modation available was incidental.

It did occur to Freeman—though he kept his own counsel for the present—that it also made it the first place the occupying force would look for any foreign nationals or money. He had started to call them "the occupying force" as he had no real idea what they were: rebels of some description? But against who, or what? They weren't Russian, although not all of them had the Caucasus genes of the Chechens they had encountered so far. Terrorists, perhaps. Again, who was the opposition as far as they were concerned? This was hardly an oppressive state, unless you were a woman. The locals had a hardline Muslim attitude to females, which had made Acquero's job as team leader hard. In passing, Freeman wondered what idiot had put a woman in charge of operations for this region. One who hadn't done much in the way of research, for sure.

Two hours after the three Americans had witnessed from the hotel window the arrival of the occupying force and the death of the police chief, they sat with their nine colleagues in the suite. They had gathered in a silence that had been long, enabling Freeman to lose himself in his thoughts.

On their initial gathering, there had been confusion and disbelief from their colleagues who had been in their rooms sleeping, working, reading, listening to their MP3 players or otherwise trying to escape their surroundings and count off the days until they could fly back to what they called real civilization. Something that now seemed to recede into infinite distance.

Once Acquero had managed to quiet them and stop their protestations at being interrupted in whatever they were doing, she had outlined the situation. And then repeated herself, angered that she had not been believed. Slaughter and Freeman had backed her up, although even they had found it hard to convey to their fellows the possible impact of events. Partly because it was all possibility. They had no absolutes to offer, and scientists and engineers dealt only in absolutes.

As they went over and over the situation, discussing what might be happening, and what could then follow from each scenario, the arguing grew less and less, until they were reduced to their current state of resigned and fearful torpor.

Freeman scanned them. Brad Simmons and Terry Callaghan were analysts and lab men who were geeks by any other name. Happier with the two-dimensional battles of superheroes than with the real-life threat of flesh and blood, they looked ashen and drawn. Con Steffans and Dieter Dierks were engineers, and looked exactly what they were: miners with a hands-on approach to problems who found no threat in the physical after facing down the elements and the soil for many years. For them, it would not be the fear of physical danger, but the oppressive weight of seemingly insurmountable logistics that bore down on them.

Isaac Obeyo and Tam Winters were engineers and geologists who worked in the spaces between the pure engineers and the pure analysts. Physical opposites, the squat, muscular Obeyo and the willowy, wiry Winters looked an odd couple, but had been chosen as they had worked well in the field together in other locations. That left three men: Evan Leonard, Mike Avallone and Peter Rattenbury. The last two were also analysts and geologists who doubled as IT techs. It was Leonard who was the enigma. A lean, graying man in his forties, he looked fitter than any of them. And although he was supposed to be a data analyst, as far as Freeman could see, he knew jackshit about data, let alone having the ability to analyze it.

He had to be there for some kind of a reason, and from the look of him he had no right to have been as damned quiet as he had been throughout the past few hours, Freeman thought. Maybe it was time that he opened his mouth.

"Hey, Leonard," Freeman said, momentarily taken aback at how loud and harsh his voice sounded in the quiet room…and how scared.

"Uh-huh?" Leonard looked at him, his amused gaze leveled at the younger man.

"You—you're a brother like me, yeah?" Freeman waited for the older man to agree, hoping that he would make the task easier. No such luck. He pressed on. "This is a serious situation we've got here, and I'm thinking that you're not that great a data analyst. Now either you made a late and very poor career change, or you haven't exactly been on the level with the guys."

"Or with me," Acquero added. "We've been carrying you, and I don't get any response from Billings when I bring it up. Like none at all."

"That's because I've been assigned to run shotgun to you idiots, and Billings, who is an even bigger fool than all of you put together, has been told by his superiors to keep his mouth shut." In contrast to the contempt of his words, Leonard's tone was even and calm.

"Then shouldn't you be doing something?" Slaughter asked.

"Like what?" Steffans interjected with contempt for the young analyst. "He's one man."

"Dude has got it in one," Leonard said. "You think I'm Superman or something? It doesn't work like that. You want me to be blunt? Most of you would be as much use as a fart in a thunderstorm. There are twelve of us. Five would be carrying seven. That's a big task under any circumstance. Right now, all I have to go on is what I've heard. It sounds like there are a lot of soldiers out there, at least some of whom know what they're doing. The best thing we can do is sit tight and play dumb until we find out just what is going down here. They might want nothing from us, in which case we can negotiate a way out. We have nothing valuable—"

"Unless they have a notion of what we've found, or even that we work for a company with a hell of a lot of cash," Slaughter stated.

"We're Americans. In some places that's enough," Simmons said miserably.

"Maybe, but not here," Leonard said with confidence. "Russia has too big a hold on this part of the world, still. A couple of decades back you might have had a worry. But not now. Now, we just sit tight and wait for the cards to fall."

BROGNOLA WASTED LITTLE time leave-taking the congressman. Arriving at his office, he contacted Billings and this time approached the conversation in a completely different manner.

Detailing his discussion with MacManus, he let the company executive know that he was out of his depth, but that his concerns would be noted. For any further action to be taken—should it be deemed necessary—it would be essential that he receive full company dossiers on the twelve members of the party. It was only when Billings hesitated, and had to be pushed, that he admitted they already had a security man on the team.

"At what point were you going to mention that? Or were you only going to send eleven dossiers and hope that I couldn't count?" the big Fed asked with as much sarcasm as he could muster.

"I thought you might not want to get involved if you knew we had already taken precautions…at least, get involved so soon," Billings replied hesitantly. "I mean, he's good. He used to be a Company man—maybe you know him?"

"I work for the Justice Department," Brognola said with a sigh. "You watch too much TV, Billings. 'Company man.' Jesus. Just send me all twelve dossiers electronically, and make it quick."

Billings was a rattled man. They were in Brognola's in-box within ten minutes, and he was already reading off the screen when he put a call through to Aaron "the Bear" Kurtzman, head of the cybernetics team at Stony Man Farm.

The Farm was the covert home base of the Sensitive Operations Group, and America's ultra-secret action teams Phoenix Force and Able Team. In addition to being high up in the Justice Department, Brognola was SOG's director. That fact was known to very few people, one of whom was the President of the United States.

"Bear, I have had a bad day already, and I need to you to run some checks and surveillance for me…" Briefly he outlined the situation as it had unfolded for him that day, ending with, "I need you to keep a watch on Chechnya and any activity inside the borders. It might be Russian, but maybe not. I just don't know. It might not even be worth our time and trouble."

There was a pause and the big Fed had a sudden feeling that his last sentence had been way off the money.

"Hal," Kurtzman said carefully, "I don't want to do anything to up your blood pressure, but before we talk any more, just take a look at the Russia Today channel…"

Brognola had a screen mounted in one corner of the office. He picked up the remote and hit the on switch, skimming to Russia Today.

He cursed softly. This day was getting worse with every minute.

4

"In essence, you are very easy to control. En passant, that is always the problem with the Chechen people—they are easy to control because no matter how belligerent they may be as individuals, you get them in a mass and they have no direction and are unwilling to take orders. And so it is easy for any force, of any size, to take them down.

"But I digress. You are easy to control in this situation because you are a small town in a position that is at once your strength and weakness. It needed just a little thought to see this and envisage a way in which to gain control simply and easily. Which I have done. All that I require now is your co-operation, which you will of course give lest you wish to be responsible for the deaths of many of your citizens. This you will not want. We will be gone from here when victory is ours, and any casualties left behind will be ones that you—and your behavior—will be held responsible for in the long term. Do I make myself clear?"

Alexsandr Orlov ceased pacing up and down in front of the battered oak desk and turned to fix Aslan Bargishev with a glare that was part intense, part mad.

Bargishev shifted uneasily in his seat. He wanted to tell this robe-clad maniac to shut up and get the hell out of his office. The two men flanking the door with AK-47s made him think better of that tactic. Bargishev was a simple man. If he wanted something, he took it. That had been how he had acquired Lev Maskhadov's wife, and his business. Maskhadov himself had gone on a "business trip" and never come back. The local council had been next. The acquired business gave him money, which was a highly prized commodity in such a poor region. The fact that a simple grain importer could also bring in crates of ordnance with the bags of grains had stood him in good stead with those in the region who realized that in a State that was still in the early stages of growth, ordnance was the real currency.

Bargishev had used his cunning, brains and oily charm to rise to the top. He had power, and he had the police chief in his pocket. The fact that the man was Mrs. Maskhadov's moron of a brother and so fond of power that he would do anything he could to hold on to it was a strongly mitigating factor.

If this man staring at him, waiting for an answer, was telling the truth, then at least the stupidity of his brother-in-law would no longer trouble him. But that was scant consolation for the rest of what this madman was spouting.

"Forgive me, for I am a simple man," Bargishev began, opting for the approach that usually gained him a foot-hold—and maybe some time, in this instance, to work out just what was going on—with any new acquaintance of use or power. "I am the humble mayor, so to speak, of this town. I sit here, on administrative business, when my phone starts to ring—both my phones start to ring," he added, indicating his cell phone and the landline on his desk, "and I am told about vehicles coming into town, and men with guns. We do not have guns around here, sir, we are a peaceful community—"

Orlov barked a harsh laugh that cut off the mayor mid-flow. "You think I'm stupid? You cretin, I have bought arms that have come through your hands. I am Chechen like you, I know what we do. Do not try to be clever, for you are not. Not as clever as you think. It was easy to take this town, and it will be easy for me to replace you while we are here. You have a simple option. Work with me, or never have the luxury of breathing to work again."

Aslan Bargishev was not the idiot that Orlov painted him. He was a liar, fraud, criminal, kidnapper, murderer and adulterer—the last being the real crime in this community—but he was not stupid. He hadn't taken the calculated risks that he had to end up clumped over his desk with his brains dirtying the window behind him.

"Fair enough. Tell me what it is that you want."

The taking of Argun-Martan had been simple. Its strength and weakness was its isolation. In the shadow of the mountains, its one winding road was easily defensible, and by the same token easy to secure. This was a time of peace, or at least as much of a peace as ever existed in the region. The Russians who still held nominal grip over the State as a whole were smart enough to know that in this part of the country a lighter hand would yield better results. They were also smart enough to realize that their very presence was resented.

So it was that the small party of Russian soldiers annexed to the town had their barracks on the northern approach. A cinder-block building that had been built in the prime of the Soviet regime, it had running water and little else, with any luxuries added since powered by a generator that ran from outside the building, and plumbed and wired in with more enthusiasm than skill.

No Russian liked being given the Argun-Martan beat, despite the stark beauty of the land. The rising mountains, the cloud-spattered skies and the harsh roar of the river amounted to nothing when a person was freezing at four in the morning in winter.

Nothing ever seemed to happen in Argun-Martan, either. The four soldiers who populated the detachment passed their tour of duty in a haze of homemade vodka. Their main goal seemed to be persuading the local prostitutes that they were not entirely bad and that their money was good.

They were bored, slack and ripe for the taking. Orlov had ordered surveillance that revealed a routine of ineptitude. An advance party of one—Viktor Adamenko— had made short work of them. One had died while on sentry duty, a giant hand crushing the soldier's cries in his windpipe, as a Tekna knife punched through his thick coat and into his kidneys. The dead man's duty partner had been dozing in a truck when a face at the window made him jump. He was about to berate his companion for waking him when a hand punched through the glass and stunned him. Before he had a chance to react, the door was wrenched open and he was on the ground, tasting the bitter dirt and moss of the roadside. It was the last thing he tasted before the relentless stamping combat boot of the giant crushed his skull, and kept pounding until it was pulped.

The remaining two soldiers had been easier. With no one left to raise an alarm or to react to one, Adamenko could make as much noise as he wished. He considered killing the generator first, perhaps to give them some notice that there was a situation, and to make some sport for himself. But no. Alexsandr had told him to make it quick, so that they could proceed according to plan.

The giant sighed to himself. This was too easy, and he liked a degree of challenge with his killing. It made it interesting. No matter. There would be plenty of other Russians he could kill slowly.

The cinder-block building had four windows and a front and back entrance. Adamenko opted for the front. He figured that these idiots were so slack that they would just leave it unlocked.

He was right; he strolled into the block as though he was resident, into a fug of tobacco and marijuana smoke. Inside was messy, unmilitary. One man was asleep on a bunk, so comatose that even the sound of Adamenko's entry did not wake him. The other was glassy-eyed in front of the plasma TV screen that was bolted to the side wall, transfixed as he watched three men take on a woman old enough to be their mother. She was yelling in Russian, cursing and urging them on. It just reinforced Adamenko's view of the Russians as worse than animals. This behavior was intolerable in a soldier. He strode up to the soldier, unleathering his Glock and setting it to short bursts. He was standing over the soldier before the man looked up, glassy-eyed. His reactions slowed by many intoxicants, he opened his mouth to ask a question when Adamenko tapped a 3-shot burst into his chest. The soldier howled with pain and fell off his chair, rolling and screaming while the giant turned to the sleeping man. He would be no fun. Even the loud burst of gunfire had not roused him. With a sigh that was part frustration and part sadness that the military was so debased, Adamenko put the Glock to the man's temple and tapped. The volley of three shots removed the sleeping soldier from this world and to a longer rest.

Turning back, he saw that the soldier with the chest wounds had pulled himself toward his own bunk and was clawing for a weapon. Maddened by the pain, his duty spurred him toward what could only ever be an act of hollow revenge. He would soon die from blood loss, but he could at least try to take his killer with him.

Adamenko walked casually across the room. Another tap took out the plasma screen, which was starting to annoy him. A flicker of a smile ghosted across his grim features. This man at least showed some signs of spirit. It was a redeeming feature that the giant would not have expected a few moments before.

As the soldier rummaged desperately among the scattered junk on the bunk, Adamenko stood and waited. He could not grant too much time, as he was on a schedule, but he felt that he could at least give the man a chance.

Finally the soldier's hand closed on the only weapon he had strength enough to hold. One hand was pressed pointlessly to a wound in his upper chest, and in his free hand he held a Walther PPK, which trembled as he arced around to cover the giant. It took all the strength he had left, and he could not even spare the presence of mind to wonder why the giant had not fired on him.

Adamenko smiled and raised the Glock slowly. "Go well into the next world," he said softly in a guttural voice damaged in childhood by the gas. "You are a better man than I thought, and showed courage."

The soldier knew he was a dead man. He squeezed the trigger of the Walther, hoping that at least he could avenge himself in death. He mustered just enough strength to trigger the pistol. His shot went high and wide, his already shaky grip kicked back by the recoil, his arm flailing as his body was driven backward by the momentum of his killer's short tap, the three rounds punching into his head.

Adamenko looked around in the sudden quiet, grunting with satisfaction at a job well done, and soon left to rejoin the main group.

With the scant military presence eradicated, it was a

simple matter to proceed into the town. There were a few farms in the region, but these were scattered as it was not prime farming land. Most of the population worked either in trade within the town, or were involved in construction as the old Soviet-era buildings were renovated or pulled down to make way for new ones. Others had more shady occupations, but these for the most part also kept them within the confines of the town. It was a self-contained community, which was one of the reasons Orlov had chosen it.

The convoy swept along the road, meeting no oncoming traffic. Just past the military post, just under three kilometers from the town itself, stood the junction box for the telephone landlines and the tower that had been erected to pick up satellite signals for cell phone networks.

The box for the landlines was a huge construction, botched and repaired since Soviet days, and prone even in the twenty-first century to cutting out in a manner that would not have been accepted anywhere else in the west. At this point, where the west began to blend imperceptibly into the east, anything was possible and anything was acceptable as just another example of the old ways collapsing and new money failing to step into the gap. No one would notice or care if the landlines went down—at least not for some time—and no alarm would be raised. The cell phone tower was another matter. The newer technology was more reliable and more relied upon; it would soon be noticed if the service was unavailable.

Orlov stationed two men with synchronized watches at the junction box and tower. Their orders were simple: at a specified time, set by the distance and speed to the town center, they were to cut the landline connections so that they were killed completely. The cell phone tower was to be temporarily disabled. Although he had no use for the landline, the phone and internet connections afforded by good cell coverage would be invaluable to Orlov's plan. The two men were engineers, specifically trained for tasks of this nature.

With communication to the outside world to be severed at a set point, and for as long as he deemed necessary, Orlov was content that he would be able to carry out his mission without any real problem.

On the sweep into the town, they encountered no resistance or query. There were some curious glances from those they passed, but old habits died hard and people preferred not to die at all until old age claimed them. The hard years of Soviet dominance, and the equally unflinching eye of the Russian state since dissolution, had built in a tendency to look the other way.

The town itself was an odd mix of buildings contained within an equally strange and irregular layout. The main street, around which the older part of town had been initially seeded, was composed of old Georgian-style buildings that were ornate and set in their own small grounds, with the retail and business premises crammed toward one end, their irregular skyline bespeaking of a hurried and unplanned construction. Gables, sharp angles and terraces made for a mix of shapes that were confusing to the eye, with the two hotels housed in the town set almost dead center. One was little more than a bar glorified by rooms above that were furnished in a most basic style. The other was the luxury hotel—maybe so by Russian rural standards, but distinctly old-fashioned and almost nineteenth century by Western European measure—in which the mining party was housed.

If they hoped that Orlov did not know of their presence, they were hoping in vain. His target town had been picked for some time, but his schedule had altered to accommodate intel reports. Their presence, even without knowledge of what they had discovered, would only add weight to his demands.

Beyond this, the town sprawled out a little into utilitarian and faceless Soviet blocks, drab and characterless dwellings interspersed with industrial units that were now dormant and semiderelict, livened only in places by the attempts of entrepreneurs to rebuild and remodel. Even these efforts dwindled to a desultory end, with the town not so much ending as sputtering to a disinterested halt.

After Adamenko had whetted the edge of his anger with the police chief, it had been simple for Orlov to dispatch men to each end of the town to secure observation posts. Meanwhile, he took the rest of his men to the administrative center of the town, where his consultation with the mayor had been as satisfactory as his knowledge of the corrupt businessman had suggested.

Having left instructions with the mayor as to how the people of the town should be informed of the changes, along with regulations concerning the curfew and restrictions he would now have imposed, Orlov deputed two men to accompany the official as he fulfilled his instructions.

So far, all was going to plan. It had been easier than he had supposed, and had more than fulfilled his hopes for success. He was a suspicious man and took this as an omen.

Of course, he had told the mayor only part of his plan. The idea of setting up Argun-Martan as an independent state within Chechnya as an example for others, so that his message could be spread, was the idealistic side of his scheme. The other aspect would only alarm the mayor, and so, by inference, the people of the town. Orlov did not want this; at least, not yet.

There were matters that he had to attend to first, not

the least of which was to establish communications with the outside world. His men carried old-fashioned walkie-talkies, which in the mountainous region proved more reliable than other, satellite-based comm systems. He deputed a man to send messages to the men at the junction box and cell phone tower: the jamming system on the tower could be lifted and connections restored.

Satisfied now that things were as he wished them at this stage of the operation, he took Adamenko to one side.

"My friend, it is time for us to visit the hotel and the interesting guests who reside there."

"Russians?" growled the giant with a vulpine grin.

Orlov shook his head. "No, my friend, better than that… Americans."

5

It took just one call to raise an alarm in Moscow. The mayor recited the message provided by Orlov over his cell phone.

"The town of Argun-Martan is now under the control and leadership of the Chechen National Socialists. We seek to show with this occupation that a true collective state of pure Chechen people can operate as an entity that does not need, or pay homage to, the Russian supposed masters. We have within our land a wealth of resources that we can utilize to build a country of which we can be proud. We have the forces and arms to mount a defense of our new state should the Russian oppressors seek to crush us. If they are foolish enough to make such an attempt, they will be shown up for the charlatans that they truly are.

"We urge that other towns and cities within Chechnya— starting with that which should lead the way, Grozny— follow our lead and join with us. Those who seek to follow will find us open to sharing our way with them. Together we can forge a new land, starting with trade links that have been denied us for so long. We have within our town representatives of a great American company who are willing to negotiate for the resources we have. We will, of course, do all that we can to keep them close and protected while we hold these discussions."

The call was delivered directly to the secretariat responsible for former Soviet states that now fell under the protection of Moscow. It was, of course, recorded, and the digital file was soon in the phones and hard drives of every person in the chain of responsibility that led directly to the president. What none of these people knew was the reaction of Aslan Bargishev when he had finished delivering this speech and the connection was dead. Up to that point he had been so intent on becoming familiar with the speech, unnerved by the gun held far too close to his head for comfort, that the full import of it had not hit him. Now it did.

"Hey, you moron, is your boss some kind of madman? Why does he want to anger the president so bad? He's more or less telling him to come and get us if he thinks he's big enough. Does your boss want to die? Because I don't!"

"This is just in, and I think that you should listen to it immediately," the government official said, barely keeping the tremor from his voice as the GI-clad president stood and walked from the dojo, leaving his opponent prone on the mat. He scowled at the interrupting official as he took the proffered phone and listened to the message, his scowl deepening as it progressed. When it had finished, he listened to it again, grunting and nodding at salient points before looking at the phone, then throwing it at the wall with enough force to shatter the instrument.

"Who are these Americans?" he snapped. Stammering, the official told him about the survey expedition. "Who authorized this?" he snapped again.

"Uh, you, sir…ultimately," the official said hesitantly. "It went through the appropriate channels, and you did see the final agreement draft…"

"Find the son of a bitch who made the draft and bring

him to me. I want the full details. This is no ordinary rebel uprising."

"Sir?"

"This bastard is inviting me to attack him and threatening the Americans by implication. 'Keep them close and protected'? 'We have the arms to defend ourselves from attack'? He wants a fight. Very well, he may get what he wishes, and live to regret it, if he lives at all. But first I want to know why he's doing this. In the meantime we need to keep this quiet while we map a strategy."

The official sucked in his breath. "That may be a little difficult, sir. Those hackers we have been trying to trace…"

The president swore with a greater force and venom than the official thought possible. He was also very dubious if any hacker would be able to do the things of which the president accused them.…

"I TAKE IT you have seen this idiocy on television?" the State Department official said to Hal Brognola.

"Seen it? I wish I'd dreamed it," the big Fed replied. "I think I did. Russia Today makes Fox News look like CNN. They've already made a circus out of it. I hate to think what they'd make a circus into."

The State Department official winced. "Colorful, Hal, but spare me. I'm not in the mood."

"Neither am I," Brognola growled, "but what do you expect me to do about it?"

"Wait until MacManus gets here," the official said softly.

Brognola waited impatiently. Despite the temperature outside, the heat in the room was turned up high, the windows closed, and he could feel the sweat gathering. He felt uncomfortable in his clothes, and this reflected his mood, making him more and more tetchy. Finally he said, "Ted, why do we have to wait for Dec?"

"Because it's his interests that are in part responsible for this," Ted Rumnell answered. "I want to know just what they had in mind for a situation like this."

"As I hear it, they didn't envisage it."

"Bullshit, if you'll excuse my language, Hal. They're greedy, but not stupid. They must at least have a security man on the inside."

"I wish I had your faith," Brognola grumbled.

Thankfully for the big Fed's temper, they didn't have to wait long before the congressman was shown into the office by Rumnell's secretary. He greeted them as she withdrew, and then commented on the heat.

"It's this way because of my health," Rumnell snapped, "and will remain so. It's nothing compared to the heat you're going to have to suffer if this goes fugazi on us. Suppose we cut the crap. Have your lobbyists told you everything? How do you know that they have? And what exactly did they have in mind by way of security for the survey party? You can answer them all at once if you wish. Or if you have any sense."

Brognola suppressed a smile. It was exactly how he would have liked to talk to MacManus, but his long acquaintance—and perhaps more importantly the fact that in the chain of command Brognola, at least on the surface, ranked far below the congressman—had put up a barrier to this. Rumnell, outranking MacManus by far, had no such obstacles.

The congressman cleared his throat and ran through the details he had given Brognola. Everything tallied; there was nothing new. MacManus had little to add about the security man who traveled with the party, other than revealing that he traveled as a data analyst.

"He can't do much on his own, but if he was known to the enemy, then he'd be useless. As it is, he may still have some use."

"Should we be talking about them as the enemy?" Mac-Manus asked hesitantly. "At the moment, this is a Chechen against Russian stand-off situation. Our people may need protection or extraction, but they're still innocent bystanders."

"No one is innocent," Rumnell murmured. "I assume that the Russian government knows exactly why permission was asked for the presence of the survey party?" He waited in vain for an answer from the squirming congressman. "I see," he continued. "What pretense did your lobbyists work under?"

"Sir, I resent your tone," MacManus blustered. "The lobby system is one that has been fostered under democracy—the like of which they do not have where the survey party have gone—for business and government to work together—"

Rumnell held up a hand. "Spare me, Dec. I'm not the press. I know the good points, but I also know the bad points. How much did they tell the Russians?"

The congressman sucked in his breath. "Because Chechnya is known generally to have mineral wealth, this was represented as the first of a number of surveys across the territory to present our conglomerate—and by extension the Russian government, with whom we would share information gathered—with a clearer picture of the distribution of the resources throughout the state."

"You never mentioned your pet Russkie?" Rumnell asked.

"I think the days of such terms are long since past, and in bad taste," the congressman said sententiously, searching for some moral high ground. "But no, we did not mention the report we had. That would have raised issues regarding the provenance of the information—"

"And meant that the Russian president would have edged in one of his pet oligarchs first," Rumnell finished. "Naturally… You do, of course, realize that the terrorists who have taken over the town will question your team? And frankly, it won't take much for them to spill whatever they know. They're lambs to the slaughter, and you should be ashamed of yourself and the people you take 'expenses' from, Dec. Not just because you've put those poor guys in an untenable situation, but because you've landed the U.S. government deep in shit. The terrorists will use this as a bargaining tool, and when the Russian president realizes that his boys have been kept in the dark about this, then that's when the shit we're in will hit that fan and splatter. We'll all get stained, Dec."

"Listen, Dec," Brognola growled, "if the Russians and the Chechens want to face each other down, then that's their business. If our people are innocent bystanders, then we can make representations to the Russians through regular channels to secure our people or try to assist. If our people are not innocent bystanders, and are in some way implicated with activities against the Russian government, even if it has no direct link with the terrorists, then we can do jackshit except watch it unfold and try for damage control when it blows up."

"You think I don't know that?" The congressman shrugged helplessly.

The big Fed shook his head sadly. "I thought that was why you gave that asshole Billings my line. Not just for diplomatic channels."

MacManus looked puzzled. "Hal, I know you have the President's attention whenever you want it. Maybe he can put men in the field. I wanted your advice, and for you to be ready when it blows up, which it inevitably will. But now you're telling me that doesn't matter as you can't do anything about it."

"Dec, let me put it this way. There are times when the constitution can only be upheld by actions taken in manner that may appear unconstitutional. At those times, people like Ted go suddenly deaf, and I claim not to know about someone who may just appear at the precipitation of action."

Brognola and Rumnell exchanged glances. The big Fed said, "I can't work out if you're being obtuse, stupid or playing safe, or maybe a bit of all three. Officially, I'm informing you that I will ask the President to have men on standby if a situation develops, dependent on the actions of both the Chechen terrorists and the Russian authorities. Leave it at that, don't ask questions and don't let that asshole Billings call me again. Now, if you'll excuse me, gentlemen, I have work to do."

IT TOOK LESS than two hours before the survey team found out what was happening. On the advice of Leonard, they stayed in the one room, with Freeman and Acquero keeping an eye on activity in the street below.

There was little to report. For the most part, people went about their business much as usual, with a stoic acceptance and reluctance to curiosity that was alien to the Americans, but had kept the Chechens alive through the decades. The only marked difference between this and any day was that the corpse of the police chief lay in the street where the giant had left it. The convoy had driven around it, and the police had not returned to collect their dead. It was only after some time that an unmarked hatchback drove up and two men in dark suits picked the body from where it lay, bundled it into the rear of the vehicle with little ceremony and drove off with little trace of the bloodless death left behind. If they hadn't seen it happen, Freeman, Acquero and Slaughter may not have believed it had happened themselves.

The only sign that anything had changed was the appearance in pairs of the tribally clad men who had arrived in the convoy. Carrying slung AK-47s , they passed at regular intervals. There were two pairs, and after an hour and a half it was obvious that they were patrolling in regular circuits.

"I want you to remember one thing," Leonard said softly to the assembled party. "We are all—all of us—innocent bystanders in this. We are simply here on business. We just want to do our work and leave. And we know nothing. We have found nothing," he added with a slow and deliberate emphasis. "We're passing through, and we want to keep our heads down and go home. Our government will be working with the Russians to get us out, so we need to keep calm."

He looked around. Although some of the team seemed to be stoic and accepting of what was going on, there were others who looked as though their fears were weighing on them. He would have expected Simmons and Callaghan to be fearful, but Winters was a surprise to him. The seemingly hard-bitten engineer was quiet and morose, and seemed to have withdrawn from the others, sitting in a corner alone.

As the others talked quietly to one another, Leonard took the opportunity to go over to the engineer.

"Hey, man, I need you to keep it together here. I need you all to keep it together," he added by way of reassurance, "and I know you're a tough dude who's seen some shit. C'mon…"

Winters laughed bitterly. "I got married last year, and

we're expecting a daughter in March. I'm getting old, and I never thought that would happen. I agreed to do this job for the bonus for her. I didn't want to miss any of her growing up. I feel pretty sick about this…"

Leonard didn't know what to say. He did know one thing, however: this made Winters an unexpected weak link.

"Shit, incoming," Freeman said from his post at the window. "That big fucker and the blond guy who pulls his strings… I have a bad feeling about this."

Leonard wanted to prepare his people, but there was little time. Before he had even gathered his own thoughts, the door to the suite was flung open.

The blond man entered, with Viktor looming over his shoulder.

"I am Alexsandr Orlov. I must say it's very convenient of you to have already gathered yourselves together. It saves me sending Viktor to do this. Now, as I have you all here I will come to the point. We are the Chechen National Socialists, and we now run Argun-Martan. If you think your government will come and save you, then you are mistaken. They will not have the choice, for we are entered into a dialogue with the Russians, which will preclude American action. This means that you are isolated, so it will be as well for you to be honest. We will need your expertise if we are to take advantage of what you have found."

Acquero, who was still nominally manager even though way out of her depth, spoke nervously, heeding an encouraging but barely noticeable nod from Leonard.

"We haven't found anything. Not yet. We've only just begun our survey, and this is just the first stop on our Chechen mission. This is a speculative trip—"

"Please, do you think I am a fool?" Orlov questioned

coldly. "I know why you are here, and if you have conducted your survey, I wish to know the results. If you have not finished, then my men will accompany you as you complete your task."

"I don't think you understand," Acquero said, trying to keep the fear from her voice. "We haven't found anything, and there's no guarantee—"

Orlov sighed heavily. Before anyone had a chance to react, he moved swiftly and grabbed the nearest member of the party—Callaghan—and pulled him so that he fell nearer to the grasp of the giant. As Adamenko pulled him to his feet, the man was sobbing and gibbering softly.

"Don't worry, I am not going to ask you to tell me," Orlov said softly.

"Thank you," Callaghan whispered.

Orlov snapped his fingers and Adamenko held the young man up in one giant fist while he leveled his Glock with the other. Callaghan's eyes widened as he realized what Orlov had really meant: one trigger pull from the giant and the young man's head was blown from his neck, the mess hitting Winters and Leonard, the twitching corpse still held upright by the giant's paw.

"Now, we do not fool around anymore. He will be the first, and he will be the last if you tell me. If not, I will have Viktor eliminate you one by one until either I am told the truth, or I have no choice but to find it out from the papers you will leave as your sole legacy.

"Do I make myself clear?"

6

Mack Bolan, aka the Executioner, set up the tripod and assisted the young man as he assembled the four-foot length that constituted the Dragunov sniper rifle. The Russian rifle had an accuracy in trained hands that was second to none, but in a combat situation, it was something that the soldier preferred to use sparingly. The lack of mobility made it a fixed point that could easily be traced back, and in such a situation as this he was unwilling to leave his men exposed in such a way.

He was heading up a six-man party who had a simple mission: to eliminate Hector Chavez, the Peruvian crime boss, and get the hell out of Lima before the local law enforcement caught up with them. This was a task not made easier by the fact that they had been forced to enter the country separately at different points, then assemble and keep a close watch on any activity that may lead to suspicion. Bolan preferred to work alone, but for this mission the powers that be had determined a team was needed.

The Peruvian government, like many in South and Central America, was keen to stamp on the crime bosses who had reduced many of their cities to nothing more than playgrounds and combat zones for personal and business grudges. However, money was a driving force, especially in economies that were otherwise starved of such a force, and the contrapull of a black economy that pumped so much into the local retail and wholesale infrastructure while at the same time providing a living for so many who would otherwise starve, made a complete crackdown both difficult and unwise. People did not want to give up their living, and if they did, then how would the party responsible for their starvation ever hope to win their votes? The fact that many of those in the civil service, law enforcement and the governments themselves added to their own incomes with sweeteners from the men they professed to be against was another mitigating factor in this almost-phony war.

Chavez was only one of those crime bosses, but he was one who was proving to be thorn in the side of the homeland. He had developed a Messianic tendency as a result of the largesse his dirty money bestowed on the populace, and he was building up to becoming the first crime boss to openly defy the law and run for president as an independent. The U.S. Embassy had kept its ear to the ground and reported that there was a groundswell of support that, even if it did not bring him victory, would at the very least prove him a viable public and political figure.

If this was to be the case, then it could possibly create a domino effect across the whole of South and Central America that would be unprecedented, and could lead to the U.S. having on its borders a slew of nations run by openly criminal leaders. Chavez had been an economic problem for some time; his operations had been giving the DEA a king-size headache, and without the political implications, it was obvious that a man with such clout running a drug operation into the homeland would be a logistical headache that many involved parties could well do without.

So Chavez had to be eliminated. He was a threat that

was growing, and the only way to prevent this nasty boil coming to a painful and pus-filled head was to lance it now.

There was something about missions like these that nagged at Bolan's sense of democracy, yet he also knew that only by such covert actions was it sometimes possible to maintain the equilibrium that democracy needed to grow and prosper. At the end of the day—hopefully this day and if he was still alive—the pragmatist in him held sway. Besides, the country was better off with one less crime lord. This was why he found himself in charge of five Marines who had combat experience in the Middle and Far East, and who had been hand-picked by Hal Brognola to accompany him on this mission. The landscape may change, but the tactics remained basically the same.

Rendezvous had been in Lima. Getting the ordnance into the country had been the major problem. Three of the men had come via conventional transport means, and were, to all intents and purposes, just tourists or business travelers. A day or two on their alleged business, which allowed them to scout the land, and they were ready to meet up with the others. One had traveled as a member of the embassy staff—a temporary replacement for a worker on vacation—and would return to the embassy if undetected to resume his post and assumed identity to monitor closely the situation following the—hopefully—successful result.

Bolan and Billy Symes, the man with who he was now assembling the Dragunov, had come the hard way. Over land and river with a beat-up truck that was loaded with fruit and vegetables, the ordnance stashed in compartments built into the body of the truck, the two men had braved the semi-tropical season and the hostile eye of the villagers whom they had passed. In the dense vegetation and forest that flanked the roads, it was hard to tell if they were being watched or followed, but the finally honed instincts of the solider—and the combat-sharpened senses of his companion—had given them the necessary edge.

Hijack and robbery for fruit, vegetables or a beat-up old truck was unlikely, especially as they seemed to be the worst traders known to man: when stopping to sell and maintain their cover, they struck poor deals, and word of these idiots soon spread. They were looked on as fools, and because they were known to have little money they became poor targets for robbery. By the same token, with little cash for bribery or extortion, the military and local police who may have been tempted to stop them would mutter insults and let them pass.

By such subterfuge had they reached Lima with their real cargo intact, having escaped any serious attention from potential enemies. Timed so they arrived on the day of mission delivery, they'd had no need to worry about cover stories. They'd headed straight for the rendezvous.

Reno Starrit and Gates Tymon, two of the Marines, had made contact with Rey Suarez, identified by embassy intelligence as the weak link in Chavez's chain. Making his acquaintance had been simple: he liked clubs, coke and prostitutes. Top quality, or at least as top quality as could be found in Lima. Which, to be fair, was pretty good quality for all three: there was enough crime cash floating around to subsidize a high standard. Certainly high enough to entice two alleged businessmen, in town and bored. Suarez was easy to find, and easy enough to befriend, especially as they had a war chest to buy merchandise, which they then shared with him, taking care to ensure that in truth he was the only one getting wasted.

Once he was in that condition, the resentment that had been reported started to come to the fore. He was a peon, nothing more, and treated as such by that bastard Chavez who only came from the same village. They had started out together in the crime organization, and now he was the gofer while Chavez handed out orders. His bitterness was forthcoming, as were the details pried from him without his knowing.

When he awoke in Starrit's hotel suite the next day, with a thumping head, dry mouth and the clothing of two hookers strewed around him, he was presented with cash from the war chest and a warning: his big mouth had gotten him into trouble; he had accepted cash for his betrayal. Any attempt to backtrack and plead with Chavez would only mean his own painful death while Starrit and Tymon had a chance of escape. Any attempt by Suarez to run was doomed to failure—either from the two Americans and their unspecified allies, who he wouldn't see coming, or from Chavez's men, who knew him all too well.

Faced with such a fait accompli, Suarez could only go along with the Americans. He had already detailed the drug baron's movements and habits, and now he agreed to trigger an alert that would bring the man out into the open that night, his escape plan to be—with no little irony—his death warrant.

Letting him scuttle back to his rat's nest, the Marines had linked up with their companions as planned and briefed them. In the privacy of a safehouse provided by the embassy, the six men had mapped out their actions. The execution was to be down to Symes, who was a crack shot chosen for his particular skill. Bolan was to direct the other four men as they flanked the drug baron's estate, neutralizing as many of the perimeter defenses as possible, in preparation for the moment when Suarez raised an alarm. This was to be when a routine patrol did not report in, having been eliminated by Bolan's men. Suarez knew the time they should report, and knew when he had to act. If he didn't, then his reluctance would raise suspicion when the men were inevitably found. Damned either way, he had little option but to stick to the prescribed schedule and hope he could escape detection or death in the ensuing melee, knowing that the Americans, at least, would spare him.

When twilight began to spread over Lima, the six-man party moved to their target area. They traveled in three groups of two, with Bolan and Symes taking the truck. On rendezvous, the area was secured from prying eyes and the truck's compartments swiftly unloaded. Each man was issued a FARA 83 assault rifle with folding stock and enough ammunition to reload at least three times. The folding stock made the rifle easy to carry, and its Argentinian origins had been deliberately chosen to make the source of the attack harder to trace.

For the same reason, they were also issued Chilean SAF machine pistols, the BSM/9Ml Uzi knock-off being ideal for close combat work. They also carried some concussion and smoke grenades to lay down cover, as well as Benchmade Auto Stryker knives, the four-inch Tanto blades an essential piece of equipment for the kind of stealth killing they would have to make.

Before they set off for their target, there was one last thing: the truck. It had been wired with a GPU explosive carried especially so that once the mission was under way it would detonate, providing a distraction and also eradicating as much as possible any DNA or fingerprint evidence that even the most assiduous care could not prevent.

Chavez's estate was walled in, with broken glass along the top of the walls and closed-circuit TV cameras located in the shrubbery and trees. There were also obvious CCTV cameras set on poles, but Suarez had revealed that these were dummies, designed to deter or mislead any potential intruders. Motion detectors were also set within the grounds, the regular guard having had their location drummed into them after too many accidentally triggered panics. Thus, their routes were rigidly defined and easy to intercept. Night-vision and infra-red monocular headsets made the location of their devices easy to spot and avoid.

Scaling the walls, despite their primitive but effective defense, was a simple task, the only difficulty for Bolan and Symes being to drag the broken-down sniper rifle after them. It slowed them, and by their synchronized watches they could see that they were falling behind. It was imperative they be in place by the time the initial strike was made. Although they all carried small short-wave transmitters tuned beyond the bands known to be in use, they were to be used only as a last resort.

All three teams made their way through the undergrowth, picking their way around the detectors and heading for a point where two of the teams knew they would encounter Chavez's security patrols. When the sentries hit the right point in their circuit, the Marines would be ready for them. Taking them out at these points would enable Bolan and Symes time to set up the Dragunov and sight it for the point where Chavez would make his exit.

Starrit and Tymon took out their men with ease. The guards were complacent, talking as they made a desultory patrol. It was easy for Tymon to drop down beside the lead man, one arm snaking around his neck and putting him into a lock while the other punched the Tanto blade home with one sharp and decisive motion. The guard at the rear, stunned, had no time to react as Starrit stepped out of cover behind him, his hand covering the guard's gaping mouth while his blade found the man's kidney and ripped upward.

Around the other side of the compound, Deacon Bell and Dean Sebastian, the other two Marines, carried out a similar action on their patrol. From there, the four men spread out to cover the estate as widely as possible. As that happened, Bolan and Symes finished assembling the Dragunov and the soldier moved out toward the house.

The five men would have to get into position within three minutes. Bolan moved through the foliage of the estate until he could clearly see the sprawling villa, the garage area for the drug baron's car collection and the helipad with a UH1-D Huey in place.

Symes would be concentrating his sights on the latter area. The job of Bolan and the other Marines was to keep as many bodies away from Chavez as possible, then lay down cover for escape.

The numbers counted down to zero. Inside the house there was an increase of activity, and Bolan could visualize that Suarez had raised the alarm, unable to deny the lack of guards, no matter what his fear told him to do.

Self-preservation was a wonderful instinct. Suarez acted predictably because of it, and so did the drug baron. As the level of noise and subsequent alarm within the house rose, the first of the baron's men emerged, to stand guard between the villa and the chopper. The pilot started to fire up the engine. The noise would provide excellent cover, making it hard for those near the helipad to locate with any accuracy the fire that would soon be raining down on them.

Bolan raised the assault rifle and joined the first volley of fire that was designed to pin the baron's men to the villa. Blindly, some of them began to return fire, but were spraying in all directions.

There were concealed lights within the grounds of the compound. It would have proved impossible to take them all out in the time they had. However, as they fired up, it also proved impossible for them to be of help to the baron's men. As light flooded the grounds of the compound, smoke grenades were thrown from each side of the foliage, laying down a blanket that made it hard for the gunmen to see, while their sporadic appearance through the mists was reminiscent for the Marines of shooting fish in a barrel.

In the growing chaos, three of the guards formed a phalanx around Chavez as they tried to hustle him toward the chopper. They were tight to him, but this was no obstacle for Symes, who—while chaos raged around and in front of him—took aim carefully and punched out a shot that took off the top of the drug baron's head. A neatly drawn entry hole and an exit that took most of his skull and scattered it behind him accounted for the criminal and political career of Hector Chavez. Three more tightly clustered shots, in quick succession, took out the three men around him. Then, calmly, Symes began to dissemble the rifle, waiting for Bolan to come back to him and ignoring the combat ahead.

Some of the guards, having returned to the villa and grabbed gas masks, were now cutting through the smoke and fanning out toward the grounds. They outnumbered the Marines by three to one, but had one major disadvantage: they were in plain sight as they moved out. Despite the lights, the Marines had used their knowledge of the light placements to conceal themselves. The very thing designed to highlight an enemy was now the downfall of the home forces. Switching to the subguns, wide arcs of fire either cut down or disabled the opposing forces as the Marines began their retreat. Concussion grenades saw the remaining security force decimated.

Bolan rejoined Symes, and they dragged the Dragunov back over the wall. They were joined by the other four Marines, returning the ordnance to the truck, which still had five minutes on its timer before it blew up. Everything had gone right about this mission, and as the six men split up to avoid being spotted easily, later to link up at the embassy before being flown home under diplomatic cover, Bolan could only reflect that it was rare that a mission went this well.

It was only after debriefing the next morning, as the Marines prepared to return to some much needed and deserved furlough in the U.S., that Bolan was drawn aside by an aide to the ambassador.

"Mr. Cooper," the aide said, using the Executioner's cover name, "there's a call waiting for you."

Bolan nodded and followed the man. He was expecting Hal Brognola to call for a progress report, as the big Fed was ever impatient. The soldier took the phone and greeted Brognola. The tone of his friend's voice as he answered was not, however, the congratulation on a job well done he had expected. Instead, Brognola was to the point.

"Striker, when you get back, Jack will be waiting to bring you straight to D.C. I need your help. There's a situation—"

"Hal, I need to do some work on a few things before—"

"Striker, we've got Russians and Chechens going up against each other with some American nationals getting caught in the middle. I really need your help on this one before things get ugly and our people are killed."

"Okay, you've got my attention."

7

Orlov got the Americans to clean up the mess in the suite themselves. After all, it was their fault that one of them had been killed. If only they had been more forthcoming. It was a pity that the nature of the American was such that he or she felt the need to indulge in subterfuge. If they had any brains in their heads, they would have realized that his troops arriving in Argun-Martan at this time, and his questioning of them, were not without significance; nor, indeed, prior knowledge of what they had sought and found.

They would learn. He was no engineer or chemist, and so he needed the expertise they could bring to understand the full import of their findings. This, and more importantly perhaps, the advantage to which he could turn these findings. They would have plenty of time to think about this while they were billeted in the run-down 1950s Soviet-built theater that had at one time run social realist films and uplifting dramas about tractor production, but had latterly shown any cheap Hong Kong or American action flick that had some explosions and bare breasts and could bring in a few coins.

It appealed to Orlov's sense of twisted humor, and his equally twisted sense of drama, to put them in the theater. It had a resonance for himself and Adamenko that ran on a personal level, such was his bond with the giant who had suffered in his childhood. Moreover, it would have a greater resonance and significance for the people of the town, for the people of Chechnya and for the people of Russia should their president attempt to flex his muscles and move on the town. Again, this was of great appeal to the rebel leader's sense of the dramatic: to recreate history would stir up many emotions in the people he sought to rally.

Did it do that at great risk to himself? Perhaps. There was always a chance that the Russians would feel the red mist descend and come charging in to reclaim what they saw as their territory. If they were that blind, then it would be likely that it would be goodbye Chechen National Socialists. But Orlov was a gambling man, and if there was one thing he would have bet his life on, it was the greed of the average Russian.

Orlov had baited and tempted the Russian leader with the wording of his statement. He knew that the man would be in little doubt about that. He would lure the Russian Bear into the open, and it would be roaring. It would not rest until the upstart Chechens were smashed. It would want the world to know that.

And then he would dangle the findings of the survey party in front of the eyes of the Bear.

And he would see what they would say then.

And, perhaps, what the American government would say.

Orlov relaxed back into his bath. To the Americans, the luxury suite of the hotel may have been anything but. Orlov and his men had been living rough in the Caucasus while they had been preparing for this move. A bath of any kind was luxury, let alone the best that Argun-Martan had to offer. And after this, the soft bed and the softer mayor's wife. Orlov knew the story of how the mayor had won her, and felt it fitting that he should lose her the same way. She was a pragmatist; so was the mayor. He had shrugged and allowed her to go. That way, he was still alive.

He had made the Americans clean the suite not just to hammer home the lesson. If he was going to use the suite, he did not want it to resemble a charnel house.

"BIG MAN LOOKS uneasy," Freeman murmured softly to Leonard, indicating Adamenko, who stood in the doorway to the auditorium, reeling off orders to three guards and looking nervously around. "Why would a hard-faced bastard like that get jittery here?"

Leonard did not look around, contenting himself with tidying the bedding they had been given. "It doesn't matter why, it just matters that he does. You'd better hope that he's just briefing the detail and won't be one of them. They all look a hell of a lot more in control."

"That's not saying much," Freeman said.

"I know, but we've got to take everything we can right now. I don't know why that blond asshole has got us billeted here—"

"So he can take our suites at the hotel," Freeman said bitterly.

"That isn't the reason," Leonard snapped back. "He could have put us anywhere. Why here?" There was something nagging at his memory, just out of reach.

"Well, I'll tell you one thing. I'm sure glad they didn't have fixed seating in this flea pit," Freeman said, eyeing the stacked chairs against the walls. The once polished floor was now scuffed and worn, while the walls were drab gray, maybe once white, with peeling movie posters and handwritten notices in indecipherable script scattered around. At one end of the hall was a small theater pit, now boarded over, with a raised stage that had a movie screen hanging ceiling to floor, ripped in three places. There were two exits to each side of the stage, and the main entrance into the lobby at the rear. The two smaller exits by the stage were unguarded, but had large padlocks across the bar locking system.

"I wonder what's behind the screen?" Freeman muttered.

Leonard eyed him sharply. "Don't even think about it, son. If there is a way past there and out to the back, you'd be shot down before you were even through the screen. If they only wounded you and you had the balls to keep going, without any idea of layout, they could track you down inside or just wait till you found the back and then shoot the shit out of you."

"What else can we do? Or think about?" Freeman asked, biting down on his words to prevent his voice rising with his anger.

"Surviving, son. That's what we think about. You do something stupid—I do something stupid—and it's not just you or me who gets killed. You think that freak won't delight in taking out some more of us?"

"No, he needs us," Freeman said, shaking his head. "We know shit he doesn't really understand. Our specialty is what can keep us safe."

"You really believe that? It didn't keep Callaghan alive, son. Sure, he needs some of us. Some. Maybe only one or two. That leaves lotto many of us who can bite the bullet. My job is to keep you as safe as possible, and right now, that just means alive."

"Well, you didn't do that great a job for Callaghan, did you?" Freeman whispered. "So maybe it's just every man for himself."

Leonard looked around. The rest of the team was still in shock from what had happened at the hotel, and no one was taking much notice of the two men arguing. Leonard did not blame them. It was likely that none of them had ever seen anything quite as brutal and swift as Callaghan's execution.

Acquero had complied immediately with Orlov's request, and had been at great pains to try to appease him. She now looked ashen and on the verge of vomiting, but Leonard had to admire the way in which she had tried to think on her feet and keep her people alive. He hadn't thought she had that in her. Give her the night to get past the initial shock and she might be useful. Freeman, too, maybe. The kid had balls the size of a basketball, but he needed to rein himself in, especially as the bored and disinterested-looking guards could have their attention dragged to the argumentative Freeman at any time. The last thing Leonard wanted right now was their attention.

"Listen to me. Keep your voice down or else those goons will take you on one side and give you shit now. You won't even have a chance to try to escape. You want to do that? Fine, then you stick with me. I was trained in this shit, remember? Right now, there is no chance of getting out. Just as there was no chance when we were at the hotel. You want to die? Then fine, go ahead. You want to stay alive? You want to have the chance to escape? Then listen to me now. We need to look to see what these guys do—all of it. They all have routines, and they stick to them. That's how people work. You know those, then you can find holes in them."

Freeman was breathing heavily, trying to control his temper. He looked away from Leonard, but also made sure to avoid looking at the guards. His mouth was tight as he nodded and said through clenched teeth, "Okay, I'll buy that. But how long before they go schizoid on us again?"

"That's the one thing we can't predict," Leonard admitted. "We just have to try to ride whatever luck we have. But I'll tell you this—the blond guy wants a face-off with the Russians, and from the way he was questioning us, we're his trump card."

"The Russians won't care about a few American hostages, will they?"

Leonard laughed. "No way. But think about it. This little survey was kept very quiet. You think our bosses told the Russians exactly why they wanted us here? Uh, no… If they had, then we wouldn't have been able to move for Russian scientists and the military crawling all over us. So what the blond guy has to tell the Russians will be news to them, and it'll be very embarrassing for the U.S. government when our bosses have to come clean to them. To avoid some kind of major incident, they'll have to step in."

"Yeah, but how?" Freeman asked.

Leonard shook his head. "I wish I knew for sure. But things will move, and when they do, that's when we'll have the opportunity to act. Events make the space for action, believe me. We need to be ready. Stick with me on this."

Freeman breathed deeply. "It's hard, man. I just feel like I'm going to explode if I don't do something to try to get out. It's oppressive, like some kind of claustrophobia."

"It's okay to feel like that," Leonard said softly. "There wasn't a time on an operation that I didn't feel like that. You just need to make it work for you."

"I'll try…but what if nothing happens?"

"It will, son, it will. It has to."

BY THE TIME Bolan had reached Washington, the story had spread beyond Russia Today and had become a lead story on CNN, Fox and Sky throughout Europe. From a local conflagration between a Big Brother state and its nominally independent satellite, it had become a matter of major international diplomatic importance.

The leader of the Chechen National Socialists had been smart in ways perhaps even he didn't fully understand. His plan to tempt the Russians into confrontation and then hit them with the potential of the mineral lode would have been enough to make the Russian government pause for thought. The man had seen the American party as a part of this potential, but had likely been so focused on his corner of the world that he had failed to realize how important their presence would be on the world stage.

The U.S. had to get involved. There was no way that the government could leave the survey team unprotected and in peril. Not just because it was not the American way, but also because it sent out a message to the rest of the world that needed reiterating more than ever since the war on terror had commenced.

Bolan mulled over the current state of Russian political affairs on his way back to D.C. He kept an eye on the rolling news channels and allowed his mind to wander back over the years. He remembered the last decade of the Cold War, and the way in which it made men of a certain generation view the East and West, even now. He had to admit that there was something of that attitude in himself, fostered by the experiences he'd had with persons who had lived though those times and brought those attitudes to the fight in which he had been a participant.

One thing he knew for sure as he landed in D.C.: this would never be a one-man job. He would have to head up a team, and it wouldn't be possible to make it a team of U.S. forces like those he had just led in Peru. Down there, in a private war, it was possible to cover tracks and deny culpability if things went wrong. That would not be possible if he had to take a team across mainland Europe and land in the North Caucasus. With enemies on all sides, the chance of discovery was too great. He would need a team of locals, mercenaries who were as trustworthy as their allegiance to their salaries would allow, and who would not be swayed by the nationalist fervor on either side.

By the time he arrived at the Mall and headed for the Lincoln monument where he'd meet with Hal Brognola, he was already running through a mental catalog of names; men he could call on to take up the fight.

"Striker, you look like a man with a load on your mind," the big Fed said as he arrived, wasting no time on preamble.

"There's a lot to consider," Bolan replied, going on to outline what he would require for the mission. There were names in his head; he needed to know the necessary war chest would be available to pay for them.

"That can be arranged," Brognola agreed. "There is one thing you should know..." He went on to detail the findings of the survey team and the circumstances that had led to them being in Argun-Martan.

When he finished, Bolan sighed heavily. "If the Russians get wind of this, then they could really go to town, and there would be a lot of people around the world who wouldn't blame them."

"That's why this has to be as discreet as possible."

"What, with every news camera on the globe as close as they can get? That's a big request, Hal."

"Don't think that those responsible aren't going to be answering some awkward questions from government," Brognola said.

Bolan grinned mirthlessly. "That'll be a great consolation when someone has me in the crosshairs, Hal."

The big Fed was silent for a moment. When he did

speak, he said simply, "I wish you could have had some downtime first. I'm sorry about that."

Bolan grunted. "Rest would be good, but only to recharge the batteries. I'm good to go."

8

"I know the president likes to ride, but you would think that perhaps he would give his attention to the matter at hand and not leave us standing here like we were serfs for the czar. Oh no, I forget, he thinks he is the new czar," the Russian general grumbled as he rubbed his gloved hands and blew into them, breath misting on the air.

"General Azhkov, it would be better if you moderated your tone," the minister said softly. He cast a glance at the impassive faces of the president's guard, and the equally unmoving visages of the men accompanying the general. Why, he thought, does everyone except me have a personal guard?

He tried not to let the feeling creep from resentment to paranoia as he continued. "You may—or indeed may not—be able to rely on the discretion of your men. I leave their loyalty up to you. One thing I do know is that you should always be circumspect in the presence of the president's personal forces. One cannot be sure who is a friendly face and who will turn a deaf ear."

"Idiots," the general grunted. "He's being a pain in the ass dragging me out here when he could just call me. Pretentious bastard. If there is work to be done, then it is better that I get on with it."

The minister sighed. At least his words had, he hoped,

distanced himself from the attitude of the man who stood beside him. While the minister was a young man, still in his thirties, who had mostly grown up in the post-Soviet era, the general was only a year or two younger than the president, and had come up through the ranks during the hardest of times. The two men had crossed swords and been allies over the years, and now one was to entrust a delicate matter to the other.

Delicate was hardly a word that the minister would ascribe to the general, but maybe this was part of some elaborate payback campaign on the part of the president? Who knew? He was, at best, unfathomable at times.

The minister and Azhkov stood side by side, looking out across the Steppes on a cold and misty morning. The flat expanse of land was gray and pale green in color, with the odd splash of heather and bracken to break up the wide expanse. Firs stood in isolated copses across the vista, and from the distance they could see a party of four approaching on horseback, riding fast. In front was a bare-chested man, while those riding on his flanks were dressed in military uniform. As they came nearer, it was plain to see that the bare-chested man was the president, and as they came within touching distance before wheeling to a halt, it was possible to smell the sweat on the horses and their sour breath as they panted with their exertions. The minister flinched and stepped away, but the general stood firm, his face like stone.

The president swung himself down from the saddle, a broad grin on his face that exploded in a mirthless laugh as he clapped the general on the shoulder and then embraced him. It was not an embrace that Azhkov returned. When the president let him go, he stepped back and looked Azhkov up and down.

"Mr. President," the general finally said, " I assume you

have called me here because the matter for which you wish
to brief me is so delicate that it cannot be done in either a
civilized location, nor at a civilized time."

The president barked a laugh that this time contained
more mirth. "Sergei, as always you have the manners of a
bear with a fir tree up its ass. Of course I could brief you
elsewhere, but I wish to remind you who is in command
these days."

"I do not think I need reminding—"

"Perhaps not. But you know why you are here, and you
know why it must be you."

The general nodded. He was of Chechen descent, and
had served many years in the region when a young soldier.
"You think my past will be useful to you. Not tactically, as
you have already made up your mind how to play things.
Besides, it has been so long since I have been back… But
my parentage will look good when they speak to you on
Russia Today, yes?"

"That is partly it. There is more…" He went on to detail everything that had happened to date, including ver-
batim exchanges that he referred to the minister to supply.
When he had reached the end of his briefing, he concluded,
"The Americans make it difficult. It is on an international
stage now. But the thing that interests me is why they were
there, and what they have found. The Chechen rebels—"
he gestured dismissively "—they are paltry and can soon
be crushed. Why do they invite this? Because they have
another bargaining tool. This can only be one thing."

"A mother lode?" the general queried.

"Of course, Sergei, it can be little else. We are one of
the biggest producers of natural gas, oil, coal and electric-
ity in the world. What we have beneath our soil is what
will make us wealthy and restore the power we had in better times. Better for some more than others, but that is the

way of nature. In much the same way, we have this natural benefit—we must take advantage of it. No matter what that takes. Do you understand me?"

The general grinned. "Perfectly. As long as prying eyes can be kept far enough away."

"That can be arranged, can it not, Minister?"

The minister stuttered his agreement. He had been watching with a kind of detached bemusement, wondering if the iron curtain had fallen only in the eyes of the world, but not in actuality.

"Good," the president said with a decisive nod. "Then why are you both still here?" With which he mounted his horse, whipping its sides and yelling as he turned it, galloping back the way he had come, decisively ending the meeting. His outriders followed.

"He does not change," the general murmured as he watched the horses recede into the distance.

The minister could not bring himself to ask if this was a good or bad thing. Instead he turned and walked back to the car in which he had driven himself here, leaving the president's guard to stand firm while the general and his men returned to the limousine that had conveyed them to this spot. It was a long drive to the general's home base, and from there he would need to take his favored commanders down south by plane. It would be nearly thirty-six hours until he had his tank corps in place.

Thirty-six hours for the minister to prepare the world's press and leaders—possibly even in that order—for the events that were to come. Given the intransigence of the president and General Azhkov, and the tone of the communiqué from Argun-Martan, the minister had a sinking feeling. When he was a younger man, he had watched the disaster of October 2002, when Chechen rebels had taken the Moscow theater, resulting in military action that had been heavy-handed and had seen deaths that even then he had considered unnecessary.

There was something about the current action that baffled him. He remembered the first Chechen war from things he had read when first joining the ministry, although he had been an adolescent. Such things had not been reported when they had occurred. That had been due to an Islamic incursion into Dagestan, in support of the Shura's attempts to gain independence from Russia. It had been slapped down, but had only bubbled under until erupting into the second war, which he remembered much more clearly, and which had only really settled in the past half decade.

Both wars had really been about actions against the Russians that had taken place outside the Chechen Republic. Dagestan had taken the brunt of the first conflagration, and the second had really been spurred on by terrorist actions that Chechen separatist groups had taken, which had mostly been focused on major Russian cities, particularly Moscow. Car bombs had killed innocent civilians, and targeted actions against the populace such as the theater siege had been designed to hurt the people and make them bring pressure on the government.

Ruin their election chances rather than hit military and political targets. And it had in many ways worked, although there was a nominal independence and the "protection" of Russia, despite the overtones of such an agreement, left the Chechen Republic pretty much alone.

So why would any group seek to put its own people at risk rather than strike at the enemy? It made no sense. They had to realize that the president would not back down if it came to that point. No matter what their bargaining tool, no matter how strong they thought it might be, then surely they had to realize that they would be crushed.

Unless their advantage was that big: more mineral wealth and American nationals would put them in a pretty strong position.

Not that strong that they could afford to misjudge the president's wrath, though, and the minister feared that they had done this, and that things were going to get a whole lot worse, a whole lot more bloody, before this matter was resolved.

"OKAY," ASLAN BARGISHEV said as he stood in front of the desk that he had until so recently sat behind, "you tell me what you want, and I'll do it. No worries."

Orlov could see the sweat spangling the mayor's brow and could smell the fear coming off him. He sat back in his chair, enjoying the experience.

"There's one thing I don't understand," the mayor gabbled on. "Actually, a lot of things, but this one more than the others… What do we actually get out of this? You get the tanks come rolling down the road, but how are you going to stop them and stop the whole town from getting blown to bits?"

Orlov smiled benignly. "That, my friend, is not going to happen. Assemble the people in the meeting hall for three o'clock this afternoon and I will explain what is going to happen. We have a full hand, and there is no flush that the president can pull that will draw."

Bargishev wrinkled his brow then nodded. "Okay, boss, if you say so…"

Seeing that he was dismissed, the mayor made his way out of the building that had formerly been his domain, being allowed out by the two men who now stood guard at the entrance. Orlov's only security inside the building was his close ally, Viktor Adamenko.

As he began to make the rounds of the tradesmen in

the town, spreading the word of the meeting via their out-
lets, Bargishev mused on the man who had taken over his
office, his town, his wife. Orlov was a man who exuded
an air of confidence, and he seemed to know what he was
doing. He had a good tactical sense, as he had secured the
town with only a handful of men. They were well drilled
and, like their leader, had an air of authority about them.

If they knew as much about cards as their boss, though,
he would have to organize a few card classes before things
got too serious....

"THEY'RE UP TO something, and I wish I knew what it was,"
Slaughter said in an undertone to Acquero as they sat on
their makeshift beds in the old theater. The men guarding
them had been joined by another two who had conversed
with them in lowered voices, gesturing to the lobby, before three of the four had departed, leaving only one man
on the doors. He sat to one side, his AK-47 across his lap.
He seemed casual, perhaps too much so, but the survey
team was generally so dispirited that its members felt no
desire to test his mettle.

"If it affects us, we'll know soon enough," the woman
replied.

Since the death of Callaghan, Slaughter had not made
one single joke. His appalling one-liners had driven her
mad while they had been working together, and she hadn't
thought that she would ever miss them. But the fact that
he was now so subdued was not a good sign, and as a ba-
rometer of general morale it was too accurate for comfort.

"I'd rather know now," Slaughter said pathetically. "If
they're going to kill us, I wish they'd just do it and get it
done. I can't stand the not knowing."

Acquero took his hand. "If they were really lining us up
against the wall, you'd feel very different," she said gently.

"They need us. Killing Callaghan was for effect and to make us talk. Okay, so it worked. But whatever that psycho Orlov has planned for us and for this town, a lot of it revolves around what we've found. He doesn't know what our individual specialties are, so we just need to stick together on this. If we get a chance to do anything… Well, I trust Leonard, so we'll look to him, okay?"

Slaughter looked over at the security man. His expression revealed his uncertainty, but he had seen the way that Leonard had calmed Freeman the night before. Maybe Acquero was right.

"Okay… But I'd give anything to know what they're up to," he said hesitantly.

ARGUN-MARTAN WAS a small town, and its people had proved so far to be malleable and resigned to any kind of occupation. Although they greatly outnumbered the rebels that Orlov had bought into the town, they were conditioned by a lifetime of being under either the Soviet or Russian heel to automatically shy away from any kind of confrontation with troops. So far this had been to Orlov's advantage, but if the Russians should choose to send tanks directly into the town, then the strength of his men may be tested in more than one direction, as these people seemed to bend with the wind.

He had to persuade them that they should remain lashed to his mast, no matter what storms should beset them. He found those metaphors and similes appealing. Maybe he should use them in his speech.

The meeting house was a building that predated the stark blocks of the post-war Soviet era. It predated the revolution, and had been built in the early years of the twentieth century, its minarets and peeling paintwork in time-dulled hues of red, white, gold and black showing both the influence of the East that still dictated the religion of the town, and also the neglect into which both had fallen as the populace strove to survive in the post-Communist era.

More to the point, it was big enough to cram in the whole population, and as Orlov stood on the podium and looked out, he could see that the mayor had done his job well. Shoulder to shoulder, men, women and even children had poured into the auditorium. There was a muttering that subsided as he looked out over them, gesturing with one arm for them to be silent. Two of his men were at the back of the hall, and to one side of him was Viktor Adamenko, but as he stood in an unconscious pose that echoed Lenin, he felt certain that he would not need their presence to hold the audience in the palm of his hand. He began, his voice flowing with confidence and assurance.

"People of Argun-Martan, you stand on the threshold of making history. You may wonder why we of the Chechen National Socialists have chosen this place in which to sew the seeds of a revolution that will see us finally throw off the yolk of Russian oppression that has dogged us for so long.

"The truth is that this town is blessed—more so than any other in this glorious land. We have running beneath our feet a gift from Allah that will enable us to stand true, tall and alone. We will be the first as we have the power to defy the Russian overlords and take back our land from them. But our actions, and the wealth and power we can bring, will enable other communities to act in a similar way and so throw off not just the chains of Russian oppression, but expunge the land of the people who represent that. Chechnya is a land for Chechens, and we will eradicate—by whatever means—every trace of the Russian foe.

"All will be wealthy, in spirit as well as in material things. We will rise up. But I need you to stand tall and strong beside my men in the days to come. The Russians will bluster, but the eyes of the world will be upon us, and we cannot fail. Are you with me?"

There were mutterings and some confused glances from the floor. Orlov was frustrated. He had hoped that his meaning was clear, and certainly there were those out there that had understood him, but they were not shouting as they were forced to explain to those who had not picked up so quickly.

Bargishev jumped up onto the podium, bowing obsequiously as Adamenko growled at him. He turned to the townspeople.

"People, we have minerals under here that we can mine, sell and make us rich. If we do that with these guys, we can get rid of the Russians and kick out anyone who isn't Chechen. The Russian president—" at which he spit on the podium "—can't do anything. If we stick together, we have the power, and maybe we'll even be the new Chechen capital. To hell with those idiots in Grozny."

The muttering in the crowd grew louder until it swelled into a cheer that filled the room. Bargishev turned to Orlov.

"Okay, they're all yours."

9

"I'm glad you could join me on this one, Jack. I'm going to need a friendly face," Bolan greeted Grimaldi, shaking his hand as the Stony Man pilot entered the lobby of the Istanbul Grande Hotel.

"Sarge, I wouldn't miss this for the world. Form a bunch of guys you've never seen before into a trained unit in twelve hours and then take on the Russian military and a bunch of terrorists? When are you going to do something difficult for a change?" The pilot chuckled, then clapped the soldier on the shoulder.

"Funny guy," Bolan replied. "You know, most of the men I contacted wouldn't touch this?"

"Yeah, I had a similar experience with the ones on my part of the list. You'd think they actually saved their hard-earned cash and lived off it, instead of blowing it in bars and at card tables," Grimaldi said sardonically.

"Can't say I blame them, Jack. I need men with experience of the area as much as anything, and I guess a lot of them have reasons not to go back or get involved. Now the timetable is tighter. It's just as well Hal had you ferry me back," he added with a sly grin.

"Yeah, some coincidence," Grimaldi returned. "Listen, Sarge, the guys we've got…it worries me."

"In what way?" Bolan asked as he guided Grimaldi into a secluded seating area.

"You don't—we don't—know any of them directly. We don't know what they're like in combat. We have no experience with how loyal they are, even if the paycheck is big enough, and no idea if they're reliable in any kind of way."

"They come recommended by people we can trust. That has to be enough," Bolan replied.

"C'mon, Sarge. Sure we trust those guys, but they've only recommended personnel they know would say yes. Considering that they're saying no themselves, it kind of makes me wonder how much we can infer from that."

"Infer?" Bolan said, amused. "You've actually been writing up some reports for Hal, right? That's a very Hal word."

"Doesn't make it wrong," Grimaldi said seriously.

Bolan's tone in reply was equally serious. "No, it doesn't. I figure these aren't top fighting men. They're the best we can get, balancing reliability against willingness to go to the territory. That's why I'm glad you're here. I'll need you to watch my back, just as I'll watch yours. We've got two Chechens, three Russians and a Georgian. He'll have no ax to grind—maybe the others won't, but we should still keep it in mind—but there must be a reason why he isn't top drawer."

Grimaldi nodded. "Then we assume military discipline and look for trigger points. Got it, Sarge. Let's do it."

The two warriors got up and walked toward the conference suite where they were to meet the six men who would accompany them on the mission. It had taken time to get the names, get their agreement, and get them to this meeting place. It left little time for anything else.

Even as they walked across the lobby of the hotel, media coverage of events in Chechnya was growing in pitch and intensity. Rolling news channels demanded stories, and with the Russian military moving toward the town of Argun-Martan, that coverage was building to a hysterical pitch, predicting—though never overtly stating—a bloody showdown.

Bolan had put out calls to trusted men before setting out for Turkey, and had been frustrated by all the people who had opted out. It was not the danger that deterred; the politics of the region were a determining factor. Because he wanted men who knew the region to maximize their familiarity and save time, he had concentrated on men who had Russian or Chechen roots, or were from nearby states.

The problem, he had rapidly discovered, was that feelings on the fragile state of the region ran high on both sides of the divide, and men who usually put money above all else were suddenly discovering a sense of national pride and loyalty that maybe even surprised them.

It was only within the past three hours that he had managed to assemble a team of the size he required. Jack Grimaldi had picked him up from a NATO base in Greece, and they had flown to Istanbul in the guise of NATO emissaries sent to discuss naval placements on the Black Sea. That gave them the clearances they needed without attracting undue attention.

Bolan had picked the Istanbul Grande as, despite its name, it was a down-at-the-heel hotel that had seen better days and was off the main tourist routes. It was always busy, but with the kind of clientele who asked no questions and in return wished none asked.

As the two Americans entered the conference suite, they were greeted by six men, who swiveled from the coffee station table at the far end of the room to meet them with cool and appraising looks. Four of the men were clustered by the table, and looked as though they may have been conversing, while one stood apart and another was seated at the long table that ran the length of the room.

"Gentlemen, don't let me stop you," Bolan said with some humor. "You can speculate all you want, or you can be seated and I'll explain your mission."

"You are Cooper, of course," said the man standing apart. "You speak, so you are in command. Who is your monkey?"

"Name's Grimaldi, and if I'm his monkey, then what does that make you?" Grimaldi replied.

"The flea on your back," the man replied in lugubrious tones. He was taller than Bolan—at least six-four—and was rangy. His lean face was sunken at the jaw, and puckered skin over his left eye spoke of a time he had ducked too slowly.

"Dimitri Bulgarin. Onetime Russian lieutenant and a man with a liking for Afghanistan," Bolan said cryptically. "Yuri's description of you was accurate."

"He never liked me much. I never liked him. But he knows I work well," the Russian said. "We have all spoken, to one degree or another, but have of course been cagey about ourselves. Perhaps this is the time for you to introduce us all, seeing as you have already blown whatever cover I may have possessed."

"That seems reasonable," Bolan replied, bearing in mind the way in which the Russian tried to maneuver the psychological advantage. "Be seated, gentlemen, and we will begin."

The five fighters seated themselves along the table, joining the impassive man who was already seated. He watched them closely. Bolan noticed that although they clustered together, they still instinctively left some space between themselves and the seated mercenary. He was round-faced, with deep-set eyes and a blank expression.

He looked heavy around the middle as he sat, but his thick wrists and the thickness of his neck along with the tightness of his gray polo neck sweater showed that there was still muscle on his frame.

Bolan was in little doubt that this was Sandal Krilov, a Chechen warrior who had been allied to the freedom fighters invading Dagestan during the first Chechen war. That made him older than many of his comrades on the for-hire circuit, but his reputation was as a stone-cold killer. His allegiance to Chechnya had long since elapsed, or was so buried that he no longer cared. That he had this in his past, however, marked him as risky.

As he looked along the table, Bolan made a point of introducing the mercenaries without recourse to either asking their names or referring to the tablet that he had placed on the table in front of him. It was only when he had finished that he powered up. Meantime, he ran through the inventory partly as introduction and partly to indicate that he knew about them, could see through them.

Anatoly Vishniev, a Russian who had served both the military and the mafiya in his time, moving to whoever paid highest. He had been bodyguard and strategic enforcer to Boris Arkdhev, a banker of dubious repute to oligarchs with even worse reputations. Two months after leaving Arkhdev, the banker had been shot and killed outside his London Docklands apartment. Vishniev—a squat, scarred and unmistakable figure—had been suspected from grainy CCTV footage, but of course had an unassailable alibi, being on a Black Sea beach at the time of the shooting.

The last Russian in the group was known only as "Dostoyevsky" because of his habit of never traveling without books jammed next to his ordnance. His real name was not known, there being several aliases that had been used over the years. He was bearded, lean, silent and allegedly prone to Beserker-type rages when in combat. His background was believed to be military, and there were rumors that service in Afghanistan had been the catalyst for his going independent. Bulgarin, however, was dubious on this point, and equally as vocal.

Dzhozkhar Basayev was the second Chechen in the party. He seemed to be smiling at some private joke all the way through the briefing, his pockmarked face split by a grin. His dark eyes darted around his fellow mercenaries, as though sizing them up as much as enemies as allies. He was short, wiry and moved constantly in his seat as though unable to settle. He had spent time in Africa fighting for whoever paid highest, having left his homeland after a tangle with organized crime and a kidnapping that ended with an oligarch's daughter deflowered and dead when she should have been returned. The ransom money had also disappeared.

The last member of the party was the only one who did not give Bolan and Grimaldi too much cause for concern: the Georgian Alexei Vassilev, who sat attentive, following Bolan's introductions around the room with darting, hawk-like attention. A tall, lean man whose face was obscured by the kind of mustache worn by Georgian men twice his age, he nodded to himself as if to emphasize points made by Bolan that struck home. Vassilev had come with a high recommendation, yet there had to be a reason why he would take a mission turned down by so many. Find that out, and Bolan knew that the key to the man would be revealed.

Introductions completed, Bolan outlined to the assembled team the mission they would be expected to fulfill: to enter the Chechen Republic and secure the release of the Americans who were caught in the middle of the stand-off between the Chechen rebels and the Russian military, which was, as he spoke, advancing on Argun-Martan.

"So we work for the American government, then," Bulgarin stated rather than asked.

"This isn't a U.S.-sponsored mission," Bolan said firmly. "I've been hired by a private concern to put together a team to execute this mission." He wasn't going to directly implicate the mining consortium whose duplicity had landed the survey team in this situation, but a hint or two wouldn't hurt if any of the team chose to open their mouths, for whatever reason.

"Whatever you say," Bulgarin replied with heavy irony.

"Hey, scarface, cut the shit," Vassilev piped up. "Who cares who bankrolls this job? It's a big job, no matter what. Let Cooper outline it without the wisecracks."

This outburst extracted some amusement from the assembled team. Vassilev bowed to his comrades and gestured to Bolan to continue. Bulgarin glared at him, but held his peace.

Bolan used the tablet to call up plans and diagrams of the town, which had been provided by Stony Man Farm. The layout of the land around the edge of the Caucasus, and the territory along the river, were displayed; and the points of entry to the town and the possible strongholds of the rebels were shown. The movement of the Russian tank detachment was displayed. Anything that was known about the Chechen National Socialists was available, though that amounted to little.

Occasionally one of the men would chip in his opinion.

"This group—they are either very new or very small. I have never heard of them," Krilov remarked. "Many of the groups in Chechnya have been in existence since the first war. Not these. And the way they take their own people as hostage to the Russians? Why? Do they think they will be martyrs and this will inspire Chechnya to rise? Pah—" he gestured dismissively "—they are fools, no more than that."

"That may be true," Vishniev mused, "but does it not make them all the more dangerous? If they are this reckless, then they may make it easier to get into the town, but they will fight even when it seems pointless, and if they continue then they invite attack from outside, and this will be bad for us."

"Attack from outside is inevitable," Bulgarin added, his previous high-handed attitude for the moment dropped. "The president sends Azhkov. I have served under this man, and he is no time-waster. He will issue an ultimatum and will be eagerly counting the seconds until he can start to attack. He is not a man who likes to travel and not arrive, if you see what I mean. He likes the sound of a raging cannon."

Bolan nodded. "Then we know what we face, gentlemen. Entering the territory and attaining the target area is something over which we have some control, and will therefore be the part of the mission that we can feel confident about. Our problem will be time and the erratic nature of the two opposing forces that we have to work between."

"I trust you have a strategy for this?" Dostoyevsky said slowly.

"Gentlemen, do you think Mr. Cooper would get this group together if he didn't know what he was doing?" Grimaldi asked with a smile. "Of course he has a strategy. Take it away, Sarge."

Bolan grinned. "I have two scenarios, extrapolated from the information available, and for each of them there is a battle plan. Listen carefully, gentlemen, for we have—"

he checked his watch "—an hour before we need to leave. There will be equipment and transport ready for us at the airfield. Now...."

AN UNMARKED LIMO took them from the hotel to the airfield where *Dragonslayer* stood waiting for takeoff. They disembarked and took their places in the chopper, where ordnance supplied with one of Bolan's war chests and procured through a local contact, was waiting for them.

Before taking off, the mercenaries looked through the ordnance supplied. The guns were mostly assault rifles and SMGs, with some smaller weapons and a few larger. The grenades were flash, concussion, CS and white phosphorous, Willie Petes, with no shrapnel—working within the kinds of enclosed spaces that strategic projections gave them, these would be too risky to the civilians they had been assigned to protect. Explosives were packed, as were some Claymore mines to lay down on their retreat and slow the enemy should they be pursued. For each man there was also a blacksuit, gas mask, a pair of night-vision goggles and enough rounds of ammunition to ensure a good supply even if they sparked off a minor war.

"You are well prepared, Cooper," Basayev remarked. "I wonder if you think this will be even more difficult than you suspect. I wonder if you think we have no chance of getting out in one piece."

Bolan eyed the wiry fighter. "Any mission is a fifty-fifty prospect. Lady Luck can screw up any plan. What you do is try to even the odds and stack them your way as much as possible. You think I've been selling you a line, then you know where the door is. You'll be paid for your time so far."

"You'd go a man short?" Basayev asked, sizing up the soldier.

"Better five men at a hundred percent than six when you're carrying one who isn't."

Basayev shrugged. "For the money, I'm committed. I just don't like to be lied to when it's my ass on the line."

"My ass, too," Bolan replied. "It's fair enough to ask questions. As long as you accept the answers, that is."

"Then we understand each other," Basayev said. "I suggest your monkey—" he grinned at Grimaldi "—get this bird in the air. The sooner we get there, the sooner we get back and the sooner I get to spend this cash you're paying me, right?"

As Grimaldi lifted the chopper into the air, Bolan settled into his seat and wondered if having to accept what he could get at short notice for such a mission would be the worst situation he had ever been forced into. Looking back at the motley crew of Russians, Chechens and the Georgian, he could see not so much a group of guns for hire who could work together as a team, as a disparate group of misfits who were soldiers of fortune for no other reason than their temperaments would allow for nothing else.

That was going to make this even more of a difficult mission than he had envisioned.

10

Captain Daman Tankian had a name that caused him, with his knowledge of the English language, to smile wryly at his fate. That a military man with the first syllable of his last name should end up in a tank regiment was an irony that was not lost on him, even though he knew it would sail right over the head of the man who sat beside him, sourly staring out the window with a face that resembled nothing less than a slab of condemned meat.

General Sergei Azhkov was not an easy man to get to know, or even to get on with in the most superficial of ways, but since Tankian had joined the regiment he had found that beneath the old warrior's teak veneer there lurked a keener mind than many would give him credit for. His reputation was purely for being a hard, driven soldier. The truth was, the general had a keen interest in military and social history, and as Tankian was a graduate of Moscow University in pre-Soviet history, he had found a mutual interest that the general had cautiously breached before opening up a little more.

"General, the men are billeted and the hardware is being overhauled, ready for the morning. Are there any other orders before I stand down?"

"Yes. There is a bottle in my briefcase. Pour yourself one and pour one for me," the general said in a flat voice.

"You are off duty as far as I am concerned, Daman. All is ready for the final push tomorrow morning."

"You say that as though we rode to defeat rather than victory," Tankian remarked as he took two metal cups from the general's bag, along with a quart of vodka.

Azhkov snorted. "What is victory?"

Tankian shrugged. "An interesting question, Sergei." He handed the general his vodka. "I doubt the president would appreciate such philosophical niceties. However, I would assume that a victory in his eyes would be the routing of the rebel forces, even if it entailed leveling the town."

"Indeed. A show of force. Put the rebels in their place. As long, of course, as the Americans are saved. Which, if we adopt the kind of tactic favored by our leader, is a highly unlikely eventuality...to say the least." The general screwed up his face and shook his head before downing his vodka.

"I would hazard, Sergei, that from the way you say this, you believe that the latter is what our president would like to happen."

"He did not say so directly, of course," Azhkov replied, being as circumspect as his superior before continuing. "The rebels have good reason to be so bold. This is tied up with our foreign friends, though how is not something I know for certain. I do know that having all of them out of the way may give our leader opportunity to establish martial law."

"And under cover of this, he will be able to find out what was going on, and so profit from it," Tankian mused, pouring another measure for them both. "But the United Nations, driven as they are by American interests, will demand accountability for any casualties, no matter how incidental, or indeed accidental, they may be to the main mission."

Azhkov took the cup from his captain. "Someone will have to be the head on the block. What better way to settle old scores? I believe that, as the phrase goes, many chickens will be coming home to roost, and that an ignominious retirement and a disparaging footnote in history await me."

"Unless we can persuade the rebels to give up their hostages—that is what they are, after all—or find a way of outflanking them."

The teak face split into a grin that was as ugly as it was sardonic. Azhkov moved over to a table set in the middle of the barracks room. He used his cup to indicate the road along the river, with Argun-Martan set dead center.

"River on one side, mountain on the other. If we had infantry, then we may be able to send men to infiltrate and cut off any route of retreat. As things stand, we have been detailed to this end of the route, with no way to get our vehicles around without being seen. We cannot flank or pincer these guys. Now if another tank regiment had been sent to cover this section of road," he stated, banging down his cup on the far side of the town, "then we would be in a position of some strength. Instead, we roll in like it was Hungary 1956 and meet the same opprobrium."

"The Chechens do not even have to defend the town if they do not wish to. They can retreat, let us raze it in their wake and they win a propaganda victory."

Azhkov gestured dismissively. "They retreat and they are bombed on the road. Simple. They are fair game once they leave the civilians behind. The point is that we are the scapegoats because we have been put in that position. Like a magician, sleight of hand, smoke and mirrors…"

"Everyone looks to the tank commander who razes an innocent town and kills civilians and foreign nationals, while forgetting to ask questions about the rebels and what they had to bargain with?"

"Precisely, Daman," the general said with sad resignation. He gestured to his cup. "Pour another. In fact, let us go in search of another bottle. Tomorrow we walk into a trap that they think they have laid, while in truth it has been laid for them. And we are the terrier sent into the rabbit hole. I would rather face this drunk than sober."

"There is no way around this, Sergei?"

The general chuckled. "Not unless you believe in miracles."

Dragonslayer TOOK THE eight-man party across Turkey and into Georgia. It was a lot of territory to cover, but Grimaldi had a plan. Keep low and under the radar, steering clear of major populated areas and relying on two arranged stops along the way to refuel and check the way ahead.

When they made the first of their scheduled stops, there was some dissent in the chopper from those who wondered why, if the mission was so urgent, they would take time out.

"You guys ever hear that old proverb 'less haste, more speed'?" Grimaldi asked them. "Nah, forget it. Listen, I need to keep this baby topped up and the reserves filled. Low flying takes its toll. While I get that done, I also get to check on the local conditions. It'll get us there quicker, trust me."

Bolan always did. While the mercenaries grumbled among themselves, the soldier went with Grimaldi to meet two men manning the fuel depot. They looked like brothers. Indeed that was what they were, ex-military men who had gone AWOL and underground when the USSR had crumbled, forming part of a pipeline that smuggled weapons and outside funds to rebel groups that had fought for independence during the dark days of flux. Since then, they had made a name for themselves as security consultants for any type of business. Bolan didn't want to probe too deeply, but it was obvious from the access they had to information that some of the business concerns had links to the governments of several states in the region, including the Russians.

There was some aerial activity on the border of Georgia and Chechnya, but nothing more than usual. If there had been any leak in the activities of Grimaldi and Bolan, it had not so far reached the strategic air command of either Georgia or Russia. That much was good. It would enable the chopper to skip low across the territory and over the border with ease.

Once there, however, there were intimations of problems. Producing a laptop that was obviously wired into some places it shouldn't be, the brothers brought up a series of exchanges between air crews and ground control showing that detachments of planes had landed at the nearest airfields to Argun-Martan, ready to skirt the mountains and take out the town.

"You reckon that mad man is just going to flatten the town?" Grimaldi asked Bolan.

"Subtlety isn't his middle name, Jack. But he's not that stupid as to use a sledgehammer."

"Depends what kind of sledgehammer," one of the brothers interjected in fractured English. "Listen to this."

Another couple of clicks and they were listening to a series of communications with a tank regiment.

"That's what I would have expected," Bolan mused, "but—"

"Yeah, look," the brother said, bringing up a map of the region. He indicated the area around the town and grimaced. "Boom, yeah?"

"Oh yeah," Bolan agreed. He could see at a glance that the air strike would take place on the section of road not covered by the tank regiment. It was a setup, but who would it really benefit?

"Jack, these guys have been great, but we really need to move. When this goes down, then we need to get in, out and move fast."

When they were in the air again, he said nothing to the combat crew. Time enough for that later. The key would be in infiltrating the town and arranging an extraction that would not put *Dragonslayer* in the middle of a dogfight, which mostly depended on how much time they had.

Time: the unknown quantity that was the soldier's biggest nemesis, and one he was still considering when they made the second and final stop.

"ALEXEI, I AM WORRIED. Not enough fight, and I feel like a coiled spring. I need to release that tension or my headaches will start again. When will the Russians come?"

"Viktor, why do you wish for it so quickly? Can you not enjoy what we have begun here?"

"It is not that," the giant said with a sigh. "I do not wish to head an empire like you, Alexei. I am just a soldier. Without that, I have nothing to stop the pain."

Orlov did not know what to say. The giant had been his ally since they were children, and they had always had the same aim. But where Orlov had a dream to unite the nation and make it pure and great again, Adamenko was motivated on a much more primal level. Avenging Chechens against Russians was a simple matter for him of systematically eradicating every Russian he came across. For the most part, those contrasting views of the same aim worked well together, but as Orlov looked out of mayor's office onto the main street of Argun-Martan, he could see that the differences between them may cause problems.

Since Bargishev had helped him to get the people of

the town on Orlov's side, he had been content to let the mayor act as a kind of go-between, acting as his mouthpiece among the people as the few troops Orlov brought with him shored up the defenses of the town. It was vital that the citizens of the town be mobilized and organized into a defensive force. Orlov knew that an attack was inevitable. He had every confidence that his cards, when face up, would stop the Russians in their tracks. But first they would have to make those tracks, and when they did, the people had to be ready and protected.

Of course, Bargishev was not a trustworthy ally. The knowledge of how he attained his position and his willingness to bend to keep an eye on the main chance were ample proof of this. A Chechen National Socialist soldier was always with him, ostensibly for his protection: in truth, for Orlov's.

As for the people of the town… As he watched them build defenses and gather the arms that they kept secreted in their homes, working together with his men to build a civilian army capable of holding off the Russians for as long as it took him to reveal his whip hand, he felt a swelling sense of pride that these were his people.

Unlike Viktor, Aleksandr Orlov did not look like a native Chechen, but he was as pure as any of the people on the streets below. At least, he would have been if not for the Russian soldier who had taken his mother while his comrades forced the man he still considered his true father to watch.

The fire of Chechen nationalism burned hard within him. His father and mother had suffered in the last days of the Soviet, as Glasnost allowed the troops to run riot before they were initially withdrawn from areas that were granted independence, only to have it cruelly snatched away all too soon. The wars had scarred the landscape and the psyche of the people, which in itself was a fragile thing that had only been allowed to rebuild since the death of Stalin.

The great dictator had driven the native Chechens from their lands during the Second World War, fearing that their presence would make it hard for him to defend the Caucasus. Always a thorn in the Soviet side, the possibility of rebels taking advantage of an outside attack to further their own ends was one to which the Soviet leader was only too well aware. And so, as many other ethnic groups had been, they were displaced en masse, exiled to Kazakhstan. It was only in the late fifties, after Khrushchev's de-Stalinization of the Soviet, that they had been allowed to return.

In truth, although this exile rankled, it was also an inspiration to the young Orlov as he devoured tales of guerrilla fighters who took advantage of the siege of Stalingrad and the drain it made on Russian resources to mount an insurrection that almost achieved its aim. If not for the fact that Stalin directed Soviet bombers to Grozny rather than the Western Front, so delaying the turning of the Nazis, then there would be no need for Orlov to be standing where he was.

But history had been written a certain way; that could not be changed. What he could affect was the way in which it moved forward. If he could stop the Russians in their tracks, then he could kick-start a movement that could spread across the republic and make it truly independent once more, independent with its own wealth, the proof of which was the ace he held.

Yet for this to happen he needed the more animal impulses of Viktor Adamenko. Like Orlov, the giant was a man proud of where he came from, and he, too, yearned for a land where Chechens ruled themselves. And yet if this came to pass, then how would the giant satisfy the animal rages and impulses that drove him to kill? It was an unpleasant thought that there may come a time when his friend became a liability.

Right now, he was a driving force among the troops, and his disposal of the police chief was forgiven because the man was a foreigner by birth; not just that, but one who was also corrupt beyond even the norm of everyday life. His very presence was inspiring to the people, which was of great importance as Orlov had led them to believe that the soldiers in the town were only an expeditionary force. The truth was somewhat different: apart from a couple of men maintaining their home base, Orlov had pulled all the men his small group possessed to mount this takeover bid. He was gambling heavily, and would need all the spare manpower and motivation that his talisman warrior could provide.

It was vital that he keep Viktor happy. He clapped the giant on the back. "Do not worry, my friend. If I know the idiot president, he will be delighted to challenge us as soon as possible. Before too long, there will be many of them within your grasp. Now, tell me of our progress…"

Inwardly he heaved a sigh of relief as the giant, seemingly buoyed by Orlov's words, relayed how the civilians had begun to dig emplacements along the road on both sides of the town, laying down tank traps and mines as well as establishing observation posts they could man. Some were up in the hill farms, establishing hidden locations for what anti-aircraft ordnance they could muster. Others still were fortifying buildings within the town to use as fortresses should the Russians break through.

Plans were progressing well. Viktor was now in a happier place, the imagining of dead Russians keeping his spirits up. The town was united and ready should an attack break through, though the consensus—buoyed by the conviction of the giant when he spoke to them—was that Orlov's tactical genius would prevent this. He liked to hear those things, and it stilled the apprehension that lurked at the corners of his mind. He had planned every step, but had he considered every eventuality? He would soon find out.

The phony war was nearing an end. Soon the real battle would begin.

11

Dragonslayer was to touch down near the border between Georgia and Chechnya. There was a clearing forty klicks from the line, in treacherous territory. Grimaldi flew expertly and low amid the hills and outcrops, skirting the tops of clumped forestation, keeping just below the radar and just above being snagged by the landscape. It was a bumpy, unpleasant ride and some of the mercenaries showed signs of air sickness that amused Bolan. No matter how big, tough and strong a person was, it was a difficult façade to keep up if the inner ear told the person otherwise. The soldier had always been lucky with his, and could stomach the jumpiest of rides, which, considering some of the places he'd had to fly with Grimaldi on the stick, was a useful talent to possess.

When they touched down, he ordered the mercenaries out with an instruction to take ten, get some air and work their cramping muscles. He was aware that they had been in the air for some time, and had stayed briefly at their last stop. They would be here briefly, too, but it would be the last stop before they reached the target area and they might have to hit the ground running. If that was the case, he wanted his men as sharp as possible. While the mercenaries walked stiffly, stretching and grumbling to one another about the flight, Bolan and Grimaldi headed for a corrugated-iron and brick shack built on the edge of the clearing. It looked deserted, the sole window blacked out and the only door shut.

The shack looked as though it hadn't been used for a long time, and the clearing in which they stood was dusty, with the layer of dirt on the surface undisturbed except for their own tracks. Around the clearing, the foliage was thick, but not so much that it wouldn't show signs of recent disturbance. Bolan could see none.

The door of the shack opened slowly. The inside of the building was pitch black against the afternoon light, and the soldier's hand instinctively twitched toward the Beretta he had holstered in the small of his back. The door creaked back, and he waited with hairs bristling. Nothing happened; nobody appeared in the dark aperture.

Then, on either side of the shack, clumps of foliage moved backward as though secured on runners. Bolan realized that this was, in fact, what had been done. Cover of artificially preserved foliage that was movable to allow access with no visible trace had been placed on at least some sections of the perimeter. The runners were buried, and the soldier had to admit that he would have needed a close inspection to determine their location.

Not that this mattered now. From each newly made clearing two men appeared, one with a wheeled tank containing fuel and the other riding shotgun—or at least, an AK-47.

They stood on the perimeter, unmoving and unsmiling. At his back, Bolan could feel as much as hear the tension as the mercenaries watched what occurred and tensed.

A man limped from the darkness of the shack, leaning heavily on a cane. He was lean, lame on the left and had a face that looked like a relief map of the Caucasus, his long gray ponytail seeming to emphasize how worn he was.

"Grigory, it's been a long time. And do you have to lay on the drama?" Bolan asked. "You're scaring my man."

The old man looked at Grimaldi with a glare as stony as the mountains he resembled. Then his face cracked. As it did, Bolan could see the four men on the edge of the clearing visibly relax, as though they had been waiting for this as their sign to stand down. Equally, he could feel the tension ebb from the men behind him.

"You can never be too careful, Belasko. I tell you this when we talk, and still you don't listen." "Belasko" was an alias Bolan had used for years.

"There's careful and then there's going for an acting award," Bolan replied as he stepped forward and clapped the old man on the back. "Get your men to fuel us up. I hope you've got coffee going."

While the refueling took place, Bolan followed the old man and the Stony Man pilot into the shack. Inside presented a different proposition to the exterior. In much the same way as the entry to the clearing had been disguised, the door and window had been carefully camouflaged on the outside to appear ramshackle and neglected. From the interior, which was now lit by fluorescent lighting triggered by the old man as he entered, it could be seen that the window was a one-way mirror, with insulation designed to keep sound in as much as the weather out. The door was not the aging piece of wood it appeared to be, but in fact had insulation and security locks down a reinforced metal frame.

There was a bed, table and chair. On the table stood a tablet, a shortwave radio transmitter and a smartphone. A small stove and a kettle also stood there, with a small generator beneath the table.

Ignoring what Bolan had said, the old man took a bottle of vodka from beside the bed, fished three glasses from a tray beneath and poured three drinks. He handed one each to Grimaldi and Bolan, coughed a toast in what sounded like Russian but was too guttural for Bolan to tell and downed his glass. The two Americans followed suit.

"Good. Now we can proceed," Grigory said with a nod. He continued without preamble. "Things are not looking good. If I were you, unless you had some imperative that would mean death otherwise, I would turn back and not bother."

"We can't do that," Bolan said simply.

Grigory grunted. "I thought not. I do not say lightly that you would turn back if it were an option. From here, the flight path to Argun-Martan takes you low over the mountains, which is treacherous enough. You must add to this now the fact that there are fighters moving into the region to be based at the nearest airfield. The orders have been given. The tank regiment is in position. It is Sergei Azhkov's. You know of his reputation?"

"I've heard about him," Bolan commented.

The old man grunted. "Take everything you know and multiply by five, maybe ten. He's miserable, bloodthirsty and mean-spirited. And he'll be in a worse mood as he's smart enough to know he's being set up."

"Meaning?" Bolan queried.

"Look at this," the old man said, bringing up a map of the region on the tablet. He indicated the town and the road parallel to the river and the mountains. "Where the tanks have been situated, they have no choice but to proceed one way only. There can be no pincer movements. They move in and either eradicate the opposition or drive them back, and then into the open."

"Where an air strike can pick them off," Bolan said. "Meanwhile, the civilians get slaughtered and someone has to take the heat off the Russian president for the operation."

"Precisely. This will just make Azhkov more pissed off than he usually is, and so he will be more vicious. This makes your mission in the town more dangerous, and also makes it harder for you to enter and escape without being picked up by the increased vigilance attendant on a fighter squadron."

Grimaldi studied the map on the screen. He traced a flight path with his index finger. "If the fighters are stationed here, then they'll have to take this path across the mountains, so if I can move around here, I can avoid that corridor."

"If you are that low, then you may be seen from the farms that circle the mountains and the town," the old man counseled. With his finger, he traced a slightly different path. "Now this way, on the other hand... There is still a slight risk of being seen, but you can use some of the mountains as shelter if you feel confident of flying that low at that time."

"Are we talking about night flying?" Bolan asked. "Over that terrain?"

Grimaldi chuckled. "Evening more than night, Sarge. Even I'm not that reckless. But it will be pretty dark, and I can't risk lights."

Bolan's face quirked in a grin. "I believe you, Jack, but I think we should maybe keep this from our passengers."

"A sensible decision," Grigory agreed. "We have secured the area, and there are no overhead flights that we know of. Let your men equip themselves here, maybe eat, and then take off just before twilight so they don't have time to realize what you intend," he said wryly.

When they exited the shack, the mercenaries were in a better mood, some even laughing among themselves. Being out of the confined space and able to move had cheered them, and seeing the refueling take place brought home to them that they would soon be in action. When Bolan instructed them to retrieve their weapons from the ordnance and then get something to eat, their mood lightened even more. The apprehension of waiting and an almost interminable flight had weighed on them, and now they felt a release.

While Grimaldi helped the old man prepare rations from the supplies on the chopper, Bolan took charge of ordnance distribution. Each man had guns and ammunition, with grenades to supplement. The explosives and mines were left packed to be carried by a detail when the chopper dropped them.

"Where will Jack go after we land?" Bulgarin asked as he took charge of his weapons.

"*Dragonslayer* will come back here. His contact will have his men on standby throughout the operation, and this will be an ops post for all intents and purposes," the soldier replied.

"Does that not leave us isolated?" the Russian asked.

"Of course it does. That's what we're being paid for. You want to stay here and forfeit your payment?" Bolan said in a level tone, his eyes locked with the Russian's. He could see a flicker of doubt in Bulgarin's eyes. Doubt about the mission or about crossing the soldier? It was impossible to tell, but one thing was certain: whatever conflict Bulgarin had inside, he seemed to resolve as his eyes cleared before he looked away.

"It is only a short distance by air, I suppose," he muttered. "There is no mission that is without risk."

Bolan watched him go, realizing more than ever that he was one to watch closely. The other five mercenaries, whatever their initial qualms and clashes, seemed to be knitting together well. The necessity of having to form bonds and alliances quickly—even if only temporarily—

was something that all of them had learned, through experience if nothing else.

After the men had eaten and secured their weapons, Grimaldi checked the time and indicated to Bolan that they should wind up and depart.

Marshaling his men, Bolan got them aboard, and as the Stony Man pilot took the bird into the air, the Executioner looked down and saw Grigory's men, who had stayed out of sight while the mercenaries prepared for the coming mission, move into the clearing and remove all signs of habitation, including taking earth and scattering it over the swept areas where they had removed all signs of movement. He could see the old man limp back toward the shack, knowing that he would secure himself in there until such time as Grimaldi returned from the first leg of the mission.

Bolan relaxed and sat back. This part of the mission was the responsibility of the pilot. The team needed to get as much rest as possible before it hit the ground running.

As the chopper sped low over the ground, the trees and rocks rushing past in a blur, the light began to fade with rapidity. Back in the body of the helicopter, some of the mercenaries looked worriedly at one another and at the encroaching night beyond. Those with air sickness felt it start to creep back, and maybe not just because of the motion of the chopper.

The aircraft kept low, skimming the tops of trees and dropping even lower over those areas that were flat and barren. The moss and sparse grasses that covered the ground were typical of the lower slopes of hills and mountains in the region. Valleys and channels snaked through the terrain as walls of rock sloped gently on either side, narrowing into almost sheer rises before widening again to a safer breadth, where Grimaldi did not have to tilt the chopper to get them through with safe margins.

Somewhere around the twenty-minute mark on the journey, just as the light went from safe to treacherous, they passed over the border unseen. It took skill and experience in the poor light to negotiate some of the more narrow channels, but by steering clear of the grassier slopes that ran down the hills toward the river, they stayed away from farms that might have raised the alarm. It was a fortuitous move, as they did not know of Orlov's outlying emplacements of some of the farms nearest Argun-Martan.

"Nearing target area, Sarge," Grimaldi noted, alerting Bolan to their approach.

The soldier nodded, then left his seat to go back into the body of the chopper. Briefly, he informed the mercenaries to get ready to disembark, and while they clumsily negotiated their preparation and the roll of the chopper as it grappled with turbulence and the shifting topography below, Bolan went forward to where Grimaldi wrestled with the controls.

"ETA?" he yelled.

"Five minutes," the pilot returned as he took the chopper in as close to the town as potential eye contact and the lay of the land would allow.

Bolan checked his watch, went back and held up five fingers to the team before finishing his own preparation. Vishniev and Krilov had volunteered to carry the packs of additional ordnance with their gear, spreading the load between them. They now finished loading.

Grimaldi leveled the helicopter over the flattest piece of rock that he could find. They were in a wide valley, with an uneven floor and sparse vegetation that had at least allowed him to pick his spot without risking snaring the aircraft in trees. He lowered the chopper as far as he dared, so that it hovered only a yard or so above the rock.

Bolan slid open the door and judged the jump. It was only a short leap, but onto uneven rock. To hit it off-center could cause an ankle or leg injury that would really screw things. He poised himself then jumped. As he landed, he felt one knee take a jarring impact, but a shift of balance enabled him to keep to his feet. Once down, he was able to look up and beckon the others to follow.

Bulgarin, to his credit, seemed to be making a point by coming second, and once he was down the two men were able to lend a hand to Vishniev and Krilov as they jumped out with the extra gear. Vassilev followed. Dostoyevsky came fifth, with Basayev at the tail end. He looked none too happy at the leap, but once he had landed, stumbling slightly but held up by the man who had preceded him, he looked a lot happier.

"Worst thing," he mumbled.

"Optimist," Dostoyevsky replied before leading him to where the others had gathered, a few yards to one side of where the chopper hovered.

With his cargo now down in one piece, Grimaldi lifted *Dragonslayer* to a safer height and spun the chopper around. He would head back along his route to the relative safety of a clearing in Georgia, where he would await word from Bolan.

The solider watched him go, then took in the party who stood waiting for orders. Basayev was sighting by compass. "Town is that way," he said, gesturing. "How far?"

"Five klicks, if Jack is as accurate as always. Let's move out."

They set off in file, with Bolan at point. As they trekked over the rocky land, alert for any movement or sign of patrols from the town or from the waiting military, Bolan went over things in his mind. By the time they had covered the distance, it would be the middle of the night, which made it the right time to scout and locate their target. Depending on how much manpower the enemy had in the town, it may even be possible to secure the area and prepare the target for evacuation.

But that remained to be seen. First, they had to reach Argun-Martan without raising an alarm from either the Russians or the rebels.

12

The tank regiment was roused from their barracks by the commanding bark of General Azhkov. He had grown more and more morose as he and Tankian had sunk their reserves of vodka. He berated his junior for being Armenian rather than Russian, reasoning that he could never understand the Russian mind. What that had to do with their situation, Tankian could not fathom, and he did not hesitate to inform his superior of that. In return, Azhkov patiently explained that the Russian mind alone could explain the manner in which the Russian president had decided to scapegoat a man who had always stood by him. The Russian mind alone would understand what he was now about to do....

The general went to each barrack room in turn, screaming at his men to get themselves out on the parade ground, and now, unless they wanted to be court-martialed and shot. Hell, not even court-martialed; he would shoot them himself.

Tankian followed at a distance, drunk from trying to keep up with the general's prodigious appetite for vodka and slow to react. He watched in amazement as the general lined up his men, berated them for being idiots, slow and lazy, and then informed them that they would be moving out immediately, rather than in the morning.

"The president thinks we move at dawn. Those scum in the town think we move at dawn. We move now, we take them all by surprise."

Despite the way they had been berated, and the fact that they were being directed to move in a manner contrary to their briefing, there was no real reaction from the men. Partly because some of them, figuring they'd had a good night's sleep ahead of them, were as smashed as the general. Mostly it was because, despite his brusque manner and unfathomable rages, the general was as much like his men as any commander could be. He understood them, and in turn they understood him. They were smart enough to work out that they were being deployed in a stupid manner, and were behind the only man brave enough to give the president the finger and do things his own way.

Within minutes they were mounting their tanks. Azhkov took his position in the lead vehicle, steady despite the raving voice that betrayed his intoxication. He even deigned to assist Tankian, who was having problems ascending.

"General, it'll be dark when we reach Argun-Martan. What can we do at this time of night?"

Azhkov grinned. It seemed incongruous on his slab-of-meat face. "We can liven things up a bit," he said before giving the order to depart, his own vehicle leading the way onto the road.

AFTER DINING IN his suite at the hotel, Aleksandr Orlov decided that it would be a good time to pay a visit to the Americans. Since he'd last spoken to them, he had left them billeted in the theater with a light guard. He reasoned that they were alone, far from home and so scared that they would crap their pants rather than try to escape. He had so far been proved correct. Therefore, he was confident that his next assumption—that the discomfort they would be feeling physically and mentally would make them malleable—would also be proved correct.

Before he left his suite, he looked down on the street below. It resembled the Chechnya he remembered from childhood, rather than the peace of the past few years. The look of a town under siege, armed for defense, was comforting to him. Lurking at the edge of his consciousness, he was aware that that was not the way a born leader should think. He dismissed it from his mind. The scars of childhood could not be erased, but they could be cosmetically eased, and power would do that.

Turning away from his doubt as he turned away from the street below, he hurried to the room down the hall where he knew Viktor Adamenko would be resting—or as close to rest as his old friend could manage—and banged on the door.

"Viktor, time to pay a call on our Western friends," he yelled, hoping to make himself heard over the sound of the TV from within. A noncommittal grunt from within was the only response. Cursing quietly, Orlov opened the door.

Inside the room, Adamenko was stretched out on his bed, an empty plate by his side and a bottle of vodka in his hand. He took a long pull and indicated the TV screwed onto the wall, which blared in English.

"See? We are news, but the sly bastard only has it on the English-language channel, not the Arabic one. He does not like Muslims, I tell you."

Orlov watched the coverage. Russia Today had an English and Arabic service, to cater for the two religions and languages of business that served each end of the old Soviet Bloc. The giant was watching the English channel, where an expensively dressed woman who looked like nothing so much as a Moscow hooker was berating the

rebels while extolling the calm of the president in trying to negotiate with them, despite their noncooperation.

"You think the Americans actually believe that? Tell
me, have we heard from him? No, of course not. Lying
bastard."

"Viktor, enough for now. You know that will be shit.
He will posture and do nothing. What we have is far too
valuable for him to risk. That is why we must go and talk
to our guests."

"We?" the giant asked with interest, lifting himself off
the bed and killing the TV with the remote. The sudden
silence was welcoming.

"I want you with me. Don't bother speaking to them unless I ask you to. I think your presence may be enough. Besides, if they need more persuasion, we don't need words."

Adamenko laughed, a low, vicious growl in his throat.

ACQUERO HAD BEEN doing her best to keep her team together
since they had been in the theater, but they had been given
only basic rations and no facilities other than a screened
area by the side of the stage with a bucket that was emptied a couple of times a day. There were facilities in the
theater, but they lay beyond the guarded doors and off the
lobby. To place the guard farther back and also secure the
facilities would have been no problem. It was obviously
psychological warfare, designed to wear them down.

Only God knew why, she thought as she fingered her
rosary. They had been demoralized enough the moment
one of them was murdered in front of the others. She had
never seen anything like it, and the memory of it made
her want to vomit. In the same way, she reasoned that
they had been left alone to dwell on the murder as a way
of softening them up. The uncomfortable conditions, the
lack of information, being cut off from the world outside—

it was primitive, and realizing how obvious and basic it was should negate its effect. It didn't feel that way; it was working, and too well.

Looking around, she could see that she was not the only one affected. The engineers looked like men constrained, coiled springs that could barely contain their frustration. Leslie and Avallone kept eyeing Leonard with a kind of contempt, wondering when the Company man would show some kind of fight. She could understand their frustration, but knew that he had no option other than to bide his time.

As far as she was concerned, he had already saved Freeman's life by calming him when it looked as though he would boil over. Since then, the younger man had occupied himself by trying to rally Slaughter, who was becoming withdrawn. It wasn't really working, but at least it kept the pair of them occupied. It was Simmons who worried her the most. He was withdrawn almost to the point of catatonia. He and Callaghan had not just worked together, they had also mostly socialized as a pair. Without his friend, and having seen him murdered, he was on the verge of a breakdown.

And that was really bad. More than any of the people in the room, he was the one who truly understood the overall meaning of the test results. She knew that Orlov would be coming to see them at some point, and demand that they give him exact details. That, she realized, was a major part of his bargaining plan. If Simmons was unable to give the rebel leader what he wanted, then she was filled with dread for what might happen, regardless of any efforts their government might be making.

"DOWN THERE, RIPE and ready for the taking," Bulgarin said as he hunkered down beside Bolan on top of the ridge. The team had made good time and it was still before midnight.

The town was in lockdown, but there was no curfew evident. Bolan's Zeiss binoculars were powerful enough for him to get a good impression of the layout of the town from this distance, and to see that pedestrian and vehicular traffic was plentiful.

"Are you talking about us?" Bolan asked the Russian mercenary.

Bulgarin shook his head. "You know what I mean. Come morning, and…boom," he said dryly.

"That's exactly why we need to get in and out while it's still dark." Bolan stood, moving back from the lip of the ridge as he did so. Behind him, the remaining men were squatting or sitting, conserving energy after the forced march they had just undergone.

The path from their landing to the ridge overlooking Argun-Martan had forced them to cover a greater distance than if they had been able to travel a direct route. In between the two points lay one of the farms that dotted the region. To circumvent it they had been forced to ascend a steep hill and circle around. The weather had grown cold and windy as darkness had fallen, and the rocks had been treacherous underfoot where they'd been forced to rely on moonlight rather than risk a flashlight giving them away.

It had been slow progress, but Bolan counted them lucky that their arrival seemed to have slipped as far under the radar as Grimaldi's flight, and that during the march no one had suffered an injury that would have slowed or incapacitated him. Now, gathered on the ridge overlooking the town, Bolan was able to report his initial recce to the rest of them.

As he finished, he looked at the skyline. The mountain dipped from behind them toward the town, and a raging river dug a tunnel between their location and the rising rocks on the far shore. This formed a channel that would make it easy for a squadron of fighters to swoop down and pick off not just anything that was on the road, but anything that was on the hillside.

If they were to extract the survey party and get them to the landing zone, they would have to move them quickly over the terrain or they would be easy pickings for any fighters.

"We wait until midnight. We move before if the town gets quiet enough. I want someone watching—"

"I'll do it," Bulgarin said. "I will be vigilant. Believe me, I have no desire to hang around these hills when day breaks."

Bolan nodded and handed him the pair of binoculars. While the Russian took up position and scanned the town, the soldier gathered his men and outlined the plan of attack, using the schematics of the town on his tablet. They were to divide into three pairs and recce the possible locations where the survey party could be located.

"We know they were in the hotel. It's possible that they could still be there. There's a jail in the town police station, and there's a theater and a hotel. These are the only three locations where they could easily secure a party of that size. Each pair will check one of these locations and report on your walkie-talkies. We know the rebels can control the input and output of cell signals, so we stick to these, got it?" he said, producing his handset. "Check these now."

Krilov frowned. "Never mind that, Cooper. What the hell is making that noise?"

Bolan stooped and moved toward where Bulgarin was scanning the road into town.

"I hear you," the Russian said calmly. "It's a good thing these glasses have night vision, Cooper, but I'm wishing right now that they didn't. Come and see." He held out the binoculars for Bolan, who took them from him and followed the direction of his index finger.

What is he playing at? Bolan whispered to himself.

DUSK HAD TURNED into dark by the time that the tank regiment had traveled from its barracks to within two kilometers of Argun-Martan. Azhkov gave them the order to slow to a halt, their engines ticking over. He stood in the turret of his tank.

"When I first drove one of these," he began, patting the iron of the tank, "there was none of the help you have in them now. No computers and only the very basics of communication. I want you to think about those days. We lived or died on our wits. This is what we are going to do now. Three of us will approach by road. The rest of you will fan out and take any way around the terrain that you can to scatter their fire and to get a better angle when you fire. There will be no bombardment. I want to give them a chance to surrender, to see what they will get if they don't. I don't give a damn about what they tell the president, and neither should you. All you should care about is that we are not the stooges in their game. We are soldiers. We are fighters. And we are not fools. Now let's roll."

Retiring inside his tank, where Tankian sat still dazed and bemused by the turn of events, Azhkov settled down with a grunt beside his deputy.

"Let's show these bastards what they will get if they don't see sense."

ORLOV AND ADAMENKO had reached the front of the theater when word came through from a lookout. Orlov's cell phone rang, and Adamenko watched his friend's face darken as the call progressed.

"What is it?" he asked as Orlov terminated the call.

The rebel leader frowned. "Maybe nothing. Tanks. I think it is a show of strength to frighten us. You go ahead. Tell the Americans I will be with them and I demand answers. I will attend to this."

Adamenko nodded and entered the building, leaving Orlov to make calls to each of his outlying sentry posts.

The only sign of movement was from the road ahead, and after dispatching volunteers with antitank weapons into the field, Orlov followed the giant, feeling a little more assured.

Yet at the back of his mind, it nagged him. A tank attack by night would be incredibly stupid. Sighting would be difficult from distance, even with infra-red, and if the objective was to drive them back and not kill them, it was too great a risk. As long as they still held the Americans, any action was too great a risk. Why even make a show like this? Was it a diversion of some kind?

He dismissed the thoughts as he entered the auditorium and saw the Americans huddling together, as if for comfort, in the middle of the floor, having made a tightly enclosed encampment for themselves. They were almost cringing at the sight of Adamenko as he loomed over them.

"I think you know why I am here," Orlov began without preamble. "I have given you time to prepare, and now I need the full details of your findings and an explanation that will make it plain and simple for the cretin I have to deal with. Your futures depend on this."

Acquero stepped forward, standing in such a way that she appeared to shield her team. Again, Leonard was impressed and hoped that should they be able to make a break, she would be a strong ally. While this went through his head, what she said added to his admiration.

"Listen and listen good. I know what you want, but the truth is that the only man who can give you the kind of explanation you need is in no fit state to do that right now, and that's because your goon here killed his friend and colleague in front of him. Now, you're a fool if you think we don't want to get out of here, but a bigger fool if you think these conditions can get you what you want. I want a doctor for my man, and I want better conditions. You can only get what you want if you give us that."

Orlov smiled. It was brave speech, if foolhardy. But, looking at the man she indicated, perhaps she had a point. Perhaps he should move them back to the hotel. Precious jewels weren't to be kept in a toilet, and if they were his precious jewels in negotiation, then this place was certainly a toilet.

He was about to speak when the first shell hit home. The screeching sound of ruptured air was punctuated by a deafening explosion, with an impact that made the floor shake beneath them.

Orlov gaped. The madman was attacking? Why? It could not be; he had not planned for that.

13

As the first shell from the tank regiment was fired into the night, Bolan was already moving his men. The strategies he had formed for infiltrating the town had to be changed. With this sudden and unexpected attack, there was no chance of the kind of nighttime quiet he had hoped to use to his advantage.

However, the confusion and activity that this attack would now cause could give him a whole new cover. His men had been dressed in blacksuits, both for the ease with which they could move and carry ordnance, and also to blend into the darkness around the town.

In their packs they also carried some clothing that could be used to blend into their surroundings as civilians. In this region, any rebels or fighters usually wore traditional male Muslim dress. The majority of the population was Muslim, and the break from Russia and the old Soviet-era grip was fueled by a return to religion. This suited the mercenaries fine, as this mode of dress was light to carry and allowed them to disguise bulky weaponry if necessary.

Under orders, they changed rapidly. If they were to avoid detection as much as possible, then this was their best option.

By the time they had transformed from blacksuit-clad mercenaries to hill men who would blend with the townspeople, the first shell had caused its damage, and had been followed by two others. Down below, the town was now alive. The street lighting, which had been poor and one of their assets in the original plan, was now augmented by lights from buildings that poured, like the inhabitants, onto the streets.

"Busy down there," Bolan said, checking the streets with the binoculars. "Mostly toward the end of town where the shells hit. The jail is at that end. Bulgarin, you're taking that with me. Krilov, Dostoyevsky, you take the theater. Basayev and Vishniev, the hotel. Vassilev, I need you to move toward the tank regiment. There's going to be a lot of activity on both sides of the line, and I need intel."

"That's why we have radios," the taciturn Georgian replied. "I always get the good jobs, Cooper."

Bolan smiled. "Nothing personal. These guys are Chechen or Russian. Maybe they could have interests in the outcome that go beyond cash."

The Georgian returned the smile and nodded. "And I won't. Strictly neutral, eh?"

"Got it in one," the soldier confirmed.

As they descended around the lip of the ridge, taking the treacherous and steep hillside as fast as the uneven and loose ground would allow, Bolan scanned the area around the town. Several farms were dotted here and there, and although he had no solid information, the soldier had little doubt that the rebels would have placed men at these points to act as scouts—maybe more, if they had the ordnance. He cursed the lack of intel on the rebels, but perhaps that meant they were small, undermanned. Certainly, Krilov had been dismissive. That would, if nothing else, suggest that any manpower they had would be concentrated more toward the area of Argun-Martan that had been hit.

They moved nearer to the edge of town. Here, the

buildings were dark and empty, the people in them having moved into town and toward the conflagration. It made their progress toward the center easier. At this point, they kept together, fanning out on both sides of a street, moving quickly with one man on each side preceding the other two, establishing safety.

They moved from the functional, wider streets of the Soviet-era buildings and rapidly into the closer, more ornate and much more hazardous streets of the Georgian old town. Here, the buildings crowded together and the streets did not run straight, making reconnaissance a slower process. Here, too, there were more people. Older citizens had stayed in their homes and on hearing activity outside would venture to look out.

Bolan's team was able to pass as members of the rebel group because of their dress. Even so, the big American was glad that he had been able to muster some Chechens among his team. Krilov and Basayev were able to speak easily in the native tongue—Bolan had no real grasp, and the Russians and Georgian among them would have accents that gave them away—to reassure the people.

"Put your head in, Mother, lest these Russian pigs blow it off," Basayev called to one old woman who yelled incoherently at them. To another, he called, "Do not fret, Father. They will not do to us what they did when the Germans came calling. We will protect you—that's why we're here!"

Where Krilov was brusque, yelling simple exhortations "to get inside," Basayev was gentle and seemed to have a knack for calming the locals.

Vassilev was the first to peel away from the group. From the maps he had memorized, he knew that he could run a route that would take him to the farthest point of the town, from where he could establish a recce position to cover both sides.

They reached the town center. Bolan split away from the others, beckoning Bulgarin to follow. He had chosen to tackle the jail himself, as it would be the most dangerous exit if the survey team was there, but with his lack of language and the fact that most of the population seemed to be rushing to this point, he wondered if choosing to take the Russian with him had been a good move. No matter: the others had been briefed, and there was something about Bulgarin that still rankled, made the soldier want to keep him close.

With brief acknowledgments, knowing that their time was limited, the other four men turned and headed toward their own targets, routes memorized from the tablet.

"Just you and me, Cooper, eh?" Bulgarin said with a vulpine grin.

"It is. Stick to the plan, Bulgarin, and just remember how much they hate Russians around here," Bolan replied heavily.

"LEAVE THEM HERE," Orlov snapped as the silence following the first shell was broken by the sound of confusion out in the street. "Viktor, we're needed. And you—" he directed himself to Acquero "—we will continue this later. You are in no position to make demands." Turning, he indicated the guard on the doors to move forward and cover them as he strode past, the giant in his wake.

Inside the old theater, now alone except for one guard who was looking nervous and possibly trigger happy, the Americans cautiously exchanged glances.

"Does this mean they're coming for us?" Slaughter ventured in a querulous voice.

"That's not Americans or UN." Dierks spit. "They wouldn't come in and bomb—besides, no planes overhead. Those are tanks."

"How can you be sure?" Freeman snapped.

"Dieter's right," Leonard said quietly. "And keep it frosty, people. Laughing Boy over there may not speak the language, but he understands shouting. He looks too nervous for my liking."

"That mad man in the Kremlin is going to make an example of us," Winters said softly. "Raze the town. He doesn't like Chechen rebels. I remember Moscow."

"What happened? What do you mean?" Freeman asked.

"Chill," Leonard soothed. "That doesn't matter. The point is that this may be our chance—our only chance—to escape. The Russians either don't understand what we've found, or they don't care. But while they're doing this, and it's chaos out there, then we've got a whole load of people interested in their own skins, not ours, and all we need to do is get past this dude."

"What can we do if we manage to get out of here?" Acquero asked with a tone that was less despair, more pragmatic.

"Not much. Hide in the hills. But at least we can stay alive, and sooner or later the Russians will have to account for us. They find us, then they're the good guys, right? We stay in town, we get bombed to shit like everyone else."

Like most of the survey party, Steffans had been quiet for the whole time they had been in the theater, his fear and foreboding keeping him down. Yet now, as he looked at Leonard, and then at his companions, he could see a ray of light.

"You know something? I think he's got a point. If we stay here, we're dead anyway. At least this way we've got a chance."

Leonard watched the others as they agreed, some hesitantly, others with the same kind of renewed hope that Steffans felt. He felt his own optimism rise; they might just do it. The only weak link was Simmons, who was still almost catatonic, but there were enough of them to carry one person.

They would have to. It was that or give up and die.

ORLOV AND ADAMENKO were greeted by chaos when they hit the street. As they exited the theater, the screech and deafening blast of a second shell hit them, the ground beneath their feet shaking less than before, indicating a hit farther away.

The night was lit not only by the buildings that were coming alive as the citizens panicked, but by the fire of a building ablaze three hundred meters from where they stood. The shell had taken out most of the brickwork, leaving only a skeleton and rubble where once had been a thriving bakery, and now flames from gas pipes set aflame roared into the night, fueled by anything flammable within range.

As the two rebels stood, trying to take in what had happened, the site of the second shell erupted as gasoline stored in an adjacent garage caught. There was barely time to take this in before the third shell flew overhead and hit home. Again, there was an explosion followed by another as the initial blast ignited flammable materials close by. The three fires that lit the night sky and roared above the buildings around were markers for the range of the tanks: a first strike and a warning of what could happen should the tanks advance.

Around them, people rushed with seemingly no purpose. The shock of sudden attack had caused panic, and citizens who had seemingly settled into a pattern of acting as paramilitaries for the rebels were now frightened people, scared of losing their homes and their lives. The few rebels that Orlov had brought with him tried to rally and direct the populace, but seemed to be fighting a losing battle.

In the middle of the rush, with people wild-eyed and shouting all around them, Orlov and Adamenko stood still and silent. Both men were, in their own ways, assessing the situation. Finally, Orlov spoke.

"Viktor, take two men and try to rally the people. They look to you as strength. We need to make placements in the town, and get those fires out. Where is the fire service? Get them over there…"

"Alexei, there have only been the three."

"That's enough, isn't it?" Orlov snapped.

The giant shook his head. "No, you don't understand. If this was a bombardment, a full-scale attack, then there would be more. This is a warning."

Orlov looked at the giant. "Why? I have heard nothing. An ultimatum would surely—"

"But why a warning at night, Alexei? There is something strange happening here."

"Let me worry about that—you go," the blond rebel said decisively, pushing his companion away from him. "There is too much to be done for us both to worry."

Adamenko was a man of action, not thought, and was happy enough to comply with what his friend said. As he moved off to fulfill his orders, Orlov began to barge his way through the crowd toward the barriers his men had erected at the point where the road entered the town. It seemed from the melee as though the entire population had gravitated to this spot, drawn by fear and not knowing, and yet now some of them sought to escape, pushing back against those who still wanted to get forward, to see…who knew what?

As Orlov reached the last few buildings along the roadside, where his men had dug in emplacements to cover the road, he could see that standing back along the way was a tank regiment. They had fanned out so that they were arced from the crown of the road out over the rocky terrain on each side, bordered by the riverbank on one side and the foothills of the Caucasus on the other.

Orlov understood. They couldn't surround Argun-Martan because of its location, but they could steamroller their way through it. They had announced their presence by the warning shots, and made no attempt at concealment. On the contrary, all the tanks were lit by their spots, as if to proclaim their strength in numbers.

At the defense post that was closest to the tanks, one of his men hunkered down with two civilians. They looked scared—as they should, considering they had little weaponry that would stand against a regiment—but had stood their ground.

"Sir, I've been trying to contact you—" the rebel fighter began, gesturing with his radio. Orlov realized that his radio had been left, useless, in his rooms.

The rebel leader reached out and took the radio from his subordinate. "No matter," he grunted before switching to an open channel. Quickly he barked, "Rally all personnel to the bombardment sites. Contain and extinguish fires, secure areas. All civilians not on duty should be forced to return to their homes and wait further instruction. They will be safer there. Viktor is among you, and he has no radio. Update him, take instruction on-site from him."

Then he turned to the rebel fighter. "What happened?"

"We could hear them in the distance but not see them. They seemed to be coming for ages, but didn't get closer or come into view. I couldn't work out why until they put those lights on. That was when the first shell came over. After the third, they've just stayed there."

Orlov brooded on that. There had to be a reason why

they only fired warning shots, and why they chose to do that now, when a night attack would seem such a ridiculous option. He needed to find out why; he needed some means of communication with the regiment commander. That was him, the idiot he could see standing in the tank dead center. A sniper rifle was all he needed. With one of those, he could stop this now.

Except they would still come. Maybe more so. He would have to find a way to talk.

GENERAL AZHKOV STOOD in the turret of his tank, watching through field glasses as the three shells hit home. He grunted with pleasure at their detonation and the explosions that followed in their wake.

"That will wake them up, Daman," he said with glee, "and when they do, they will realize that the only thing they face is annihilation, unless they listen to what I say."

Tankian was rapidly sobering. The president would not be pleased with what had happened. Repercussions for their careers—maybe even their lives—would be severe. Unless… If there was some way in which this situation could be turned around. If Azhkov's intransigence and drunken mood could be spun into an inspired piece of tactics, then it might be possible to come out of this in one piece.

"Sergei," Tankian said carefully, "just what is it exactly that you want to say to them?"

Azhkov chuckled. "What I want to say to them is that if they don't give us the Americans, I will shell them into submission but make sure that their leader is still alive. Then I will take great delight in shoving my fist down his throat, grabbing his ass and pulling him inside out by it."

Tankian sucked in a sharp breath. "Sergei, I cannot in all conscience tell you that this will help matters—"

"Relax, Daman. I said that is what I would like to tell them. It is not what I will actually say, if I get the chance. They will be in shock. Attack at night, and you always have the upper hand, mentally. Your enemy starts on the back foot and struggles to get off it. They will be dazed, confused and not know which way to turn. I guarantee you that right now whoever is in charge is wondering what I am doing and why."

"I was wondering much the same myself," Tankian muttered.

Azhkov shrugged. "I am not surprised. At first, it was vodka and anger, working together, but there was also something else, Daman. I am a soldier. I have always been a soldier. It is not what I do, it is a part of me. It is me. And that me is thinking this—the president wants them dead, and wants a scapegoat to avoid condemnation by the UN. They have the Americans, which they no doubt see as their winning hand. Not even a fool like our leader would sanction the murder of U.S. nationals. They are wrong. He will do this happily, as long as he can shift blame. They cannot win, no matter what they think."

"So we need to shake them up, make them realize that they cannot win and come to some agreement."

"Exactly," Azhkov said. "Argun-Martan will be scared, people running wild. If nothing else, this should make our brave rebel leader realize that not all is as simple as he would like. He will have to make a deal if he is to come out of this with his balls still attached. He will have to speak to me. I will speak to him, tell him the truth and offer him a way out. I am not the meathead he thinks, just because I am a solider. I just love my job…and I intend to keep it."

"What if he doesn't take it?"

Azhkov shrugged. "It is his choice, Daman, and his alone."

"There is one thing, Sergei… He thinks we will shoot first, ask questions second. How the hell is he supposed to make contact?"

Azkhov laughed. "Let him figure that one out himself."

14

As Basayev and Vishniev approached the hotel, it seemed empty. Even though it was lit up, there was a quiet about it that seemed in stark contrast to the activity and noise from the other end of town.

"You think they'll be there?" the Russian asked sardonically.

Basayev grinned. "They might have been staying there, but I tell you my friend, if I took over this town I'd put my hostages somewhere dark and shitty. That's why you have hostages."

The Russian laughed. "I was thinking much the same. But still, we will keep Cooper happy...."

They entered the lobby with confidence, trusting that their dress would disarm any enemies within at least long enough for them to strike first.

Inside, the lobby was empty, with the reception desk deserted.

"This is the best Chechnya can offer? Fuck, no wonder we're in so much shit," Basayev muttered to himself. "How many stories and how many rooms?"

"Four, and twenty-four rooms," Vishniev commented, counting off the pigeon holes behind the desk. "No keys, either. We're going to have to kick them all in."

"Great. Let's hope we don't annoy anyone too much," Basayev commented dryly.

Before tackling the rooms, the two mercenaries scouted the kitchens and staff quarters behind the desk, and the basement. It was an easy recce as the rooms had been left unlocked or open, with every sign of their occupants leaving quickly when the tanks had opened fire.

"You would think that the bastard Russians firing would make our job hard—with luck, it will make it easier," the Chechen commented as they went up through the lobby and then the stairs to the first set of rooms.

"It may be to our advantage, but remember where I come from," Vishniev muttered darkly.

Basayev grinned. "Not all Russians are bastards—I was talking about the ones in tanks… Now tell me you used to be a tank commander."

"Your tongue will get you into trouble more than it will get you out," Vishniev murmured as they reached the first room. "Concentrate or it will kill you," he said tersely as he made to kick the door, gesturing the Chechen to one side.

Suddenly serious, Basayev flattened himself to one side of the door then nodded. Vishniev kicked the door savagely just below the lock, and the cheap wood splintered along the lock and jamb, the door swinging open. Basayev turned and moved in at a crouch, keeping low and sweeping across the room. The Russian followed him, covering their rear. There was only one door off this room, and at a sign from the Russian, Basayev took it: an en suite bathroom, and empty.

"One down, twenty-three left…" Vishniev grumbled.

"Then the sooner you stop moaning and we do it, the sooner we get out," Basayev returned.

Shrugging, the Russian followed the little Chechen out

of the room, and they repeated the procedure on the next room. And they continued until they had cleared the floor.

It felt like a thankless task. They were making enough noise to attract the attention of any rebels that may be in the building, but none had come to engage them, and there was no noise to indicate anyone else moving above them. It was so quiet in the building that it would have been hard to disguise any sounds of movement.

They started on the third floor with a sense of resignation. It was as though they were going through the motions, but with little prospect of any result.

They swept through the rooms quickly. At least half of them looked as though they had been empty, with those that had been in use showing signs of a quick—and unwilling—departure. Belongings were strewed around, but these had been left for some time, untended. It was obvious that the survey party had been living here, but had been shifted elsewhere.

While the third floor passed without note, when they reached the fourth, it was apparent that something was going on here. In the silence that filled the rest of the hotel, the muffled noises that came from the largest suite were amplified out of proportion. The two mercenaries exchanged puzzled glances. The squeals and muffled voices did not sound to them like either soldiers or, come to that, hostages.

Vishniev indicated to his compatriot that they take the other rooms first, and with more caution. This time, they did not kick the doors in, but tried them first. Most were unlocked, the only one that had been yielded to a piece of celluloid that Basayev had taken from another room, thief's instinct telling him it may be of use. Inside this room they found weapons and half-finished meals, with bottles of vodka and brandy beneath the bed. Vishniev's look confirmed Basayev's thoughts: this had been a rebel fighter's room. So who had the suite next door? The one from which the noises came?

Who knew? Maybe they could catch the leader in a compromising position.

Signaling to Basayev to be ready, Vishniev kicked in the door and sprayed a short burst of fire into the ceiling. Plaster dust rained down on the couple who occupied the bed. A woman, seated naked astride a man who was also naked but hidden from them, screamed and fell off both the man and the bed. Now exposed, he sat up and looked at the two mercenaries.

"I can explain this," he began. "I am Aslan Bargishev, the mayor. She is my wife, even though your boss has her. Come now, can't a man have some fun with his wife?"

The mayor was obviously an opportunist who, when chaos descended, had taken the opportunity to fool around with his wife. He seemed certain he could talk his way out of this, although even his incredible confidence wavered as Vishniev and Basayev looked at him blankly.

Mistaken for Orlov's men by their dress, they hesitated and looked at each other, puzzled. So this was where the rebel leader slept, but this man was not him. Who the hell was he, then?

They didn't have a chance to secure an explanation.

Bargishev's wife, apparently embarrassed and also wary that what she perceived as rebel fighters could lead to her own demise took action. She groped frantically under the bed.

She had a Glock halfway out when Vishniev, acting on instinct at the glint of gunmetal, tapped a 3-shot burst that ripped into her torso. Her scream of pain was cut short by blood flooding her lungs, and she fell forward.

Bargishev's mouth opened in shock, uttering a wordless cry. Without thought, he hurled himself forward at the gunman, with no consideration for his own well-being or even how he hoped to avenge his wife's murder.

He hadn't even made it off the bed before Basayev tapped a burst that ended his resistance before it had even begun.

As the deceased mayor fell onto his wife's corpse, the Chechen turned angrily to the Russian.

"What did you do that for? You want us to announce we're here?"

"Rather I do that than the bitch shoots me," Vishniev snapped back. "Anyway, they're not who we're after."

"No…" Basayev looked at the dead couple, wrinkling his nose in disgust. "Call Cooper, tell him we drew a blank and are heading back to rendezvous."

The Chechen, out the door before the Russian, paused to look back and shake his head, and took out his radio.

AT THAT MOMENT Bolan would not have particularly welcomed a call coming through. He and Bulgarin had made their way toward the location of the town jail, but had found their progress impeded by the mass of the population, milling aimless and confused. While that also worked for them in that they could lose themselves, it became a trickier proposition when they could see men dressed similarly to themselves starting to move through the crowd, breaking them up and pushing them back toward their homes. In the melee it was possible for them to pass with no one realizing that they had never seen these particular rebels before. As the real rebel fighters came close, it was almost inevitable that they would see Bolan and Bulgarin and recognize them as impostors.

Bolan indicated to the Russian that they needed to move into cover until the rebels had passed them. Bulgarin nodded, and the two men sought refuge inside a shop that had been left unlocked during the panic. Once inside, with the door shut, Bolan looked out the front window, over the display, at the passing crowds.

The shop was warm, and seemed oddly quiet after the noise outside, which was muffled by the thick brickwork. The atmosphere was warm and smelled of spices and smoked meats, some of which were hanging in hocks from the ceiling across the breadth of the store, and over the window display. The latter formed a useful piece of cover for the soldier as he watched the crowds pass by.

"What if the owner returns before we can leave?" the Russian asked.

"We bluff. If not, we put whoever it is out of action— not dead, just incommunicado," he added, eyeing the way Bulgarin held his SMG.

"Are you going soft, Cooper?" the Russian said with humor.

"No need to kill unless we have to. Noise and attention are not on my agenda," Bolan answered flatly.

"Have it your way." The Russian shrugged. "You really think we can pass as rebels? Me, maybe… You? You don't even look Russian, let alone Georgian or Chechen."

"The way I look is the least of our problems. Have you seen many rebels out there? It seems to me that somehow they've taken over with very few men, and persuaded the townspeople to go along with them. They probably know every rebel by sight. Anyone gets a good look at us, we're screwed."

Even as he spoke, he knew that the moment of truth was approaching. An old man and an old woman who clung to him for support were walking toward the shop front with the air of those about to enter. The old man was bowlegged and unsteady, but the grip he had on an AK-47 seemed strong enough. Bolan indicated to Bulgarin to move back farther into the shadows as he withdrew from the window.

As the old man and his wife entered, Bolan was aware both of their sudden stiffening and of the rustle of movement behind him. The old man started to raise the AK-47, squinting into the shadows.

"Do not do that, old man, and I will not have to act first," Bulgarin said calmly in Russian.

"You are inside the town? Your tanks are a diversion?" the old woman said sharply.

"We're not with the army, we have another job," Bolan said slowly in his accented Russian. "It doesn't involve you, and it doesn't involve them. But we can't allow you to raise an alarm."

"You'll have to go through me first," the old man said. "You look like the National Socialists, but you are not them."

"Very perceptive," Bulgarin said softly. "Don't think I wouldn't go through you, and with pleasure. But we don't have the time for diversions. So drop it unless you want your wife to end her days a widow."

Bolan stepped forward. He did not want the old man to die needlessly; perhaps more pertinently, he did not want a firefight to raise an alarm.

"He'll do it. Don't give him the excuse."

There was something in his tone that made the old man waver. As the AK-47's barrel dipped, Bolan stepped forward smartly and grabbed it, jerking it out of the old man's hands, breathing a sigh of relief that there had been no need for gunfire. Without the rifle, the old couple seemed to wilt. Bolan tossed the gun to one side and grabbed them, pushing them toward the rear of the shop. While Bulgarin covered him, he searched out rope and cloth to bind and gag them, while taking the shop keys from the old man's pocket.

Leaving them, he moved to the front of the store, looking out on the street beyond. It had now emptied significantly, and there were no rebel fighters in sight. They were three streets away from where the jail was situated and, looking at his watch, he could see that they had little time left. He covered his face as best as possible with the headdress on his Muslim clothing, gesturing to Bulgarin to do the same. Leading the way, he slipped out into the street, securing the door behind them. The old couple would be found by morning, but by then their mission here would be over, one way or another.

The night was still lit up by the fires—though they were now beginning to die down where they were being put out by groups of rebels and citizens—and by the lights in the houses and stores. These would remain, as the tension of events made it impossible to sleep. As long as the people remained behind closed doors, and those outside were occupied by the collateral damage, that would suit Bolan fine. Bulgarin, he was not so sure about. The Russian seemed to be looking for an excuse to kill.

The streets leading to the jail were deserted, and Bolan hoped that their luck would continue as far as finding their target. The entrance to the police building was unguarded, and the two mercenaries slipped inside with ease.

Inside, the building was deserted. Bolan cursed to himself. If the survey team was here, then surely there would be a guard of some kind?

"You want to check upstairs?" Bulgarin murmured. "Hang on—keep point." The Russian moved behind the counter and into the rooms behind while Bolan uneasily kept watch—uneasy both for possible rebels and for the Russian, a decided loose cannon.

Bulgarin came back, shaking his head and, without waiting, took the stairs to scout the upper floor, returning quickly.

"Cells will be down… If they're here, then that's where they will be. I'll take guard—they'll be more amenable to an American voice," the Russian said.

Bolan agreed, and took the stairs down to the basement cells.

Argun-Martan was not a big town, so did not have a large jail. Even as he hit the floor in the basement, the Executioner knew he had drawn a blank. It felt empty, with no sign of life. There were four cells, two on each side of the narrow corridor, each with a shuttered metal door that was rusting. The shutters in each squealed as he slid them open, the darkened cells beyond cold, dank and empty.

Bolan's radio crackled to life. He snatched it and answered quickly, not wanting to make too much sound. Vishniev outlined briefly their lack of luck at the hotel, omitting to mention about the dead mayor and his wife. Bolan replied that he and Bulgarin had also drawn a blank.

"We'll head for the rendezvous. You do that, too. I just hope Dostoyevsky and Krilov are having better luck."

But what about Vassilev? Their point man had been oddly silent, even though he'd have to know they would now be close to the front line.

FOR THE TWO remaining mercenaries, the progress toward the old theater had been as simple as that of the men headed for the hotel. Like them, Krilov and Dostoyevsky were moving away from the focus of panic, and found the relatively deserted streets easy to negotiate. Anyone who did appear was moving toward them, was easily seen, and as a result easy to avoid. It was only a matter of minutes before they were outside the theater.

"No guard outside? Interesting," Krilov murmured.

"Indeed, a conundrum," Dostoyevsky said dryly. "Could it be that there is one stationed inside?"

Krilov sighed. "Of course that is a possibility, but it would be stupid to allow any enemy to enter into the building before engagement."

"You assume they want to keep people out. Surely they are more likely to be wanting to keep them in?"

Krilov shrugged. "Still stupid…"

"Then easier for us," Dostoyevsky murmured, moving forward. "Come…"

They moved across the road in a crouch, despite the seeming lack of any enemy. Reaching the front of the theater, they found that the doors were unlocked. Inside, the lobby was lighted and seemingly clear. There was one piece of cover: a desk and switchboard to the left-hand side. Krilov motioned that he would head to it; the Russian covered him as he went. From there, he could see that the rest of the lobby was empty. Beyond were the double doors into the auditorium. Washrooms and cloakrooms led off the lobby, and while the Russian moved inside and kept cover, Krilov scouted them and found them empty. Coming out of the last room, he gestured to the Russian to follow him.

They found the doors to the auditorium locked. There seemed to be no noise from within, but then the doors were large, padded fire doors and would insulate well. The two mercenaries looked at each other. This was a deserted area. The theater seemed deserted, as well, and so making noise was not such a problem as it may otherwise have been.

Krilov raised his SMG and tapped a burst into the lock. Dostoyevsky followed up with a kick that swung the doors heavily open. Both men were through and fanning out, seeking cover, before they had fully opened.

And both men were pulled up short by the sight that greeted them.

The auditorium was empty apart from the belongings and bedding of the survey team, and one other thing: the corpse of a man in rebel's clothing, lay in the middle of the floor with his neck at an unnatural angle.

"Well, they were here," Krilov said slowly, "but who the fuck got here first?"

The Russian shook his head. Reaching for the radio, he said slowly, "I have no idea. But I tell you, this really screws up Cooper's plans."

15

As soon as Orlov and the giant had departed, Leonard had watched the guard left behind with a shrewd eye. It had been a long time since he had been called on to take any kind of combat action—his gig as security man for the corporation was a cakewalk compared to his previous life—but although he might be a little ring rusty he still kept himself in shape, training regularly.

He would have hoped that the U.S. government would take action, either diplomatic or some kind of extraction: in which case his job was to keep the group together and calm enough for the moment to come. The trouble was, it just didn't seem as though they were in any kind of hurry: even if they had plans, then circumstance had overtaken them.

Leonard knew that their options were limited. The best he could do was to try to get them out of town before all hell broke loose and get them into the foothills where they could shelter until the fighting died down. The Russians would need to appease the U.S., and home pressures would see some kind of U.S.-sponsored search. He was relying on that for the final stage.

This part of it was up to him, though. Looking at the group, he knew he could rely on Freeman and Acquero—who had showed depths he had not imagined, while the younger man was full of guts—and he figured that of the

remaining team members, at least half would have the cool
to respond. The question was, could they afford to carry
Winters, Slaughter and Simmons, who he had fingered as
the weak links? There was no real choice. He had to carry
them somehow, the question was really about the logistics.

That could wait. There would be no point worrying
about that if they didn't actually get out of the theater.
Right now, they had one jumpy guard standing between
them and the chaos outside in which they could get killed,
but which might just offer them the chance of escape.

Leonard moved over to Acquero, and outlined his plan
to her in low tones, aiding her in folding bedding as he
spoke. Her expression showed her doubt, but she knew
that this was their only chance, and as he moved toward
Freeman she called Obeyo and Winters over to her, ostensibly to prepare rations. As he moved, Leonard could see
the guard eyeing them nervously, as though suspicious
but unsure about who to keep under closer observation.
He was rattled, which might be dangerous if it made him
trigger happy.

Freeman listened with a poker face as Leonard muttered his rough game plan. Even when he told the older
man how relieved he was to be doing something, he still
kept his expression stony. Leonard was glad to have him
on his side, especially when he saw how the young man
encouraged the downcast Slaughter, who seemed unsure
when he first heard the plan, but soon headed across the
floor to try to talk to Simmons. The young analyst was
still almost catatonic. Slaughter was joined by Winters,
who seemed to be indicating that they should take care of
the young man between them.

Meantime, Obeyo had approached Steffans and Dierks,
the two engineers responding almost too eagerly to what he
said, forcing him to quiet them. Acquero went to join Rat-

tenbury and Avallone, speaking to them in hushed tones under guise of handing them food. They stayed calm, but their body language was itchy, ready to act.

Leonard felt a little more assured. It looked as though they had the guts to pull together more than his pessimism had allowed him to think. All the while he had been watching the guard, who had winced and trembled with each of the two successive shell bursts. Although there had been no more since then, he was expecting it. That was making him nervous and—to their advantage—distracted.

Time now, then, to put the plan into action. Although the survey team seemed to be as downtrodden as before, at first glance, there was a tension about them that meant Leonard felt the need to act quickly. Their body language was in danger of alerting the jumpy guard, whose eyes were flickering nervously across the group.

The briefest of nods, and Acquero started to cry with a pain that seemed sudden and severe. Obeyo and Freeman went to her, Obeyo beckoning to Avallone. They stood over her and then backed away to show that she was now prone on the ground.

Obeyo moved toward the guard, who backed off nervously, raising his AK-47. Obeyo shook his head, spread his hands in a gesture of supplication, and in halting Russian said, "She is ill. She needs doctor. We have no first aid."

The guard looked uncertain; he hadn't been briefed for this. He knew that she was the group leader, and that Orlov always spoke to her first. That made her important. Could he risk anything happening to her, and the wrath of his leader? He moved forward, as if to try to see what was wrong with her, to decide what action he should take. He tried to keep the group in his sight as he did so, but as Leonard had instructed, they fanned out to make this hard. Avallone and Rattenbury moved a little more than the others, taking a greater risk to catch the guard's eye.

He swung toward them, his AK-47 leveled. Acquero groaned loudly. The guard was a young man, he had little combat experience, and Leonard had guessed that, playing on it. As the young guard's attention shifted again, and the barrel of his AK-47 wavered, he had failed to notice that Leonard had moved behind him.

The security man acted with a swiftness and determination he hadn't even been sure he still had in him. He was only three feet from the guard's back, and he half stepped, half jumped, his knee catching the man in the small of his back and driving him forward as Leonard's arms closed around the guard's neck. As he hit the floor of the auditorium, a burst of fire from his rifle discharged harmlessly into the wood and concrete, throwing up chips and splinters that rained around the security man as he affirmed his grip and twisted. With a sickening crack, his neck broke. Leonard felt the man go limp beneath him, and he let go slowly, straightening.

The survey team was looking at him, at the dead guard, with blank and shocked expressions. Leonard was breathing heavily. This was the first time for some years he had been called upon to take a life, and he had forgotten how it felt. Then he saw the others, and realized that they had only ever witnessed this once before—when Callaghan had been killed by the giant. Leonard realized that he had to snap them out of it. Their reactions showed how much they would have to rely on him, no matter how much courage they found in themselves.

"Come on, remember the plan. Stick together and follow me. We can do this, people," he said with a confidence that he didn't entirely feel, picking up the discarded rifle. He had no idea what was out there, but his only hope was that the shell bursts at the other end of town had drawn most of the rebels, and maybe most of the townspeople. Empty streets would be preferable. There were a lot of people on the team, and it would be difficult to find a place to hide.

KRILOV AND DOSTOYEVSKY had to have only missed them by minutes, but it was enough for Leonard to lead the survey team away from the theater, taking a side street that ran at an angle to the alley used by the mercenaries as their sheltered approach. By the time the mordant Russian was telling Bolan that they had drawn a blank, but that the party had been at that location, Leonard was already directing his people toward the newer buildings that marked the outer reaches of Argun-Martan.

Bolan told Krilov and Dostoyevsky to stay where they were. He and Bulgarin would join them as soon as possible, and he directed Vishniev and Basayev to do the same. The target could not have gone far—the Russian reported that the body of the guard was still warm, with no rigor setting in—and so it might be possible to locate them. In such a small town, it would not take the four mercenaries on foot any time at all to catch up with the two on the scene, and by the same reckoning it was unlikely that a target group as large as the survey team could move that quickly. They may have injured, and they didn't have the experience among them to make the kind of pace achieved by the mercenaries.

While they waited for the others to reach them, the two men on-site made a brief recce to see if they could pick up a trail. There was nothing definite, but Krilov had an idea of the way he would have chosen.

He explained his theory to Bolan when the four mercenaries met up. "You have one man who knows his business. First thing is, you don't head for the river as it is open

ground all the way. You go for the foothills—nearer, more
cover. You also need plenty of cover for a big group. If I
was your man, I would take the road that leads out to the
factories. More covered space and fewer people."

"Would they know this?" Basayev asked.

"They had an ex-operative on security, and they'd been
here long enough for him to know the layout. It's a good
call." He looked at his watch. "We're tight on time if we're
going to get to the rendezvous for when Jack's in the air.
We'll have to take a chance and hope their man thinks like
you and me, Krilov."

"I sure hope so," the Chechen said. "I don't want to be
here when the Russians get serious."

As Leonard led the survey team through the streets, he
tried to keep them in the shadows as much as possible,
and to keep them together. That was no easy task, as Winters and Slaughter had problems keeping Simmons with
the others, the catatonic young man stumbling and falling behind. As well, it was hard to find adequate cover
while they were in residential streets, where the clustered
houses spilled light onto the street and gave little, if any,
cover. The only thing he was thankful for was that the shell
bursts and resulting damage had kept most of the people
toward that part of town. It had made their progress easier. Now, though, the townspeople had to have been sent
back to their homes, for as he pulled the group into cover
near a garage, a small but steady stream of people walked
past them. They were downcast, confused and complain-
ing, which was good, for it meant that they were not paying attention to whoever lurked in the shadows.

Leonard could feel his people starting to fret, and as
he looked out he could see that the stream of townspeople
showed little sign of abating.

Worse, he could see rebel fighters at the back of the crowd. Checking that they were returning to their homes? No matter: if they checked enough, they would stumble on the hidden Americans. That was if they had not already been alerted by the dead guard and the empty theater.

As silently as he could, he racked the rifle. Teeth grinding, Leonard steeled himself to his task and set himself to take on the rebels, alone if he had to.

From their position in the shadows, the survey team saw the citizens stream past them, and the rebels at the rear of them grow nearer.

Leonard sized up the first of the rebels and steadied himself.

It was only when they were virtually on top of him that he realized that they looked nothing like any of Orlov's men, and his finger slackened on the trigger.

BOLAN FOLLOWED KRILOV and Dostoyevsky as they took the lead. They moved swiftly along the winding and narrow streets, and were soon behind the straggling townspeople who were returning to their homes. That slowed them a little, as they were unwilling to barge through and engage too closely with anyone who may give them away. While the Russians and Chechens cursed the delay, Bolan used the opportunity to try to see past the crowd. He figured that they couldn't be too far behind the former hostages, and as they were both a large group and also unused to moving in such a manner, then it was likely that they would need to stop at intervals to gather stragglers. In which case they would need cover…like the shadowed area near the garage that lay just ahead of the townspeople who were slowly dispersing. Some moved past, and in the shadows the soldier was able to make out a man who stood with a rifle, in a stance that suggested he was familiar with a weapon.

Bolan called Krilov and Dostoyevsky by name, quickening his pace to come level with them.

"Ahead, in the shadows—go easy now," he murmured, moving ahead of them so that he would reach the shadows ahead of his men. As he drew closer, he could see that the man in the shadows was a black man, dressed in Western clothes, and his face broke into a grin.

"Leonard, I'm Matt Cooper, U.S. Marines. My team has come for you," he said in a voice that was low but designed to carry. It wasn't the whole truth, but there was no time for explanations. He had to hope that the security man would accept what he said, or else there would be the risk of an unnecessary exchange.

Behind Leonard, he could see that the group was agitated. Some of them broke forward, and he gestured them back even as Leonard turned to do the same, and some of the others in the party pulled at them.

"I'll get them back, give me cover," Bolan ordered his men, and as he moved into the shadows, the mercenaries took up covering positions.

"Move it, Cooper. This is unnaturally quiet. No Russian tank commander is going to keep it like this for long," Bulgarin said over his shoulder.

Bolan didn't answer. He knew the Russian was right, but his priority right now was to calm the survey team and prepare its members for the long haul out of Argun-Martan.

"I knew they'd send someone covertly, damn it," Leonard said as he clapped Bolan on the shoulder, the note of relief in his voice palpable. Bolan realized how hard it had been for the security man to keep the group together and then take this risk when the opportunity had arisen. He also realized how relieved Leonard was to have help in getting them out of town, and how relieved he was that there was a plan in place. The security man stated what had been his plan, realizing what a slender thread it had been based upon, and by the same token glad that he had not had to lie to motivate his group.

Quickly, Bolan outlined to the survey team who he was, for brevity still claiming status as a Marine, and explained why his men were Russian and Chechen, to forestall questions for which there was no time.

"We have a rendezvous, and we don't have a lot of time," he finished, addressing the group as a whole. "Your man here has done a fine job, and you've shown fortitude and courage. I'm going to have to ask you to dig deep for just a little more if we're going to get out of here. Stick together, try to move as quickly as you can."

He addressed Winters and Slaughter. "If you guys need help with the walking wounded, you have to say so straight away. This is no time for trying to play heroes. You already are. We need to work together and we need to move now."

He paused to see if the group had taken in his words, scanning their faces. He could see a hell of a lot of fright, which was understandable, but he could also see determination to get out alive. That was all he needed. With a nod of affirmation, he turned to his men.

"Let's go. Basayev, Bulgarin, you guys take point and keep it clear ahead. We'll take the route we planned. Dostoyevsky, Krilov, you guys bring up the rear and keep our tail clean. Vishniev, you keep the middle moving with Leonard and me. Let's move it."

At the back of Bolan's mind, the lack of communication from Vassilev concerned him. He had no idea if anything had happened to the Georgian. If not, then why the silence? They didn't have time to retrieve him, and if his comm unit was down, then he knew the rendezvous point. Bolan took command seriously, and at any other time would have diverted himself, or some of his forces. But looking at the personnel he had, and the size of their task, he reluctantly had to leave the Georgian to his own resources.

Snapping back to the moment, he saw that his men were on the move.

Clear about their task, and the speed with which they needed to carry it out, the survey team and the mercenaries, motivated by the soldier's clear commands, moved out with a determination that could be shattered by nothing short of total war.

16

"Alexei, what are you going to do?" Adamenko asked in a voice that was small and confused, somehow grotesque in such a giant figure.

He had joined Orlov at the front line, after the last shell had hit home and its damage had been countered as much as was possible, and had looked on while the rebel leader had stood in silence, surveying the tanks that stood in formation, as brooding and silent as the man who stood watching them. Finally, Orlov had turned away, ordering his men through the radio system to marshal the population back to their homes, where they were to await orders. To calm them, he ordered that they be told he was about to open negotiations with the Russian tank commander and issue an ultimatum of their own. He reiterated this to the people who stood at the front with him, before sending them away.

They went, but as with those who were receiving the order at one remove, they were hesitant and confused by what they were hearing. Was the rebel leader about to cave in? Was he intending to declare war—a battle that they knew they could not win against tanks with the meager weapons they had. Orlov had told them of his bargaining power, and the whip hand that he held. But being fired on by tanks that they had expected to be only a threat in preliminary negotiations had shaken their confidence.

In truth, it had shaken Orlov's. He had been confident that the Russian president would not want to risk the diplomatic incident the death of the Americans would cause. Was he planning to go ahead and take out the rebels as a lesson to others, while writing off the Americans as collateral damage, the result of rebel intransigence? Orlov had truly not thought the president so bold or so stupid—depending on point of view—as to go ahead with an attack.

Was it this, or was it just a pissed-off old tank commander going mad? Whatever, it demanded a response. And the only response was to open dialogue. A counterattack was out of the question; they didn't have the firepower.

Orlov had stormed away from the front line and back to the hotel, Adamenko in his wake. It was only when they entered the hotel that the rebel leader had the first intimation that something had gone very wrong with his plans.

All of the rooms had been opened by force. When he reached his suite, he was greeted by the sight of Bargishev and his wife, naked and dead.

"Serves him right." The giant spit. "No one messes with the National Socialists."

Orlov looked at his old friend, his temper checked only by his disbelief at what the giant was saying.

Adamenko looked puzzled. "One of our men must have caught them and taken action. You detailed a guard here, yes?"

Orlov shook his head. "Everyone was pulled to the fire control, surely you realize that? There was no one here… no one that I know of. And why would they kick open all the doors…?"

With a sudden panicked look, the rebel leader beckoned to Adamenko to follow him. He rushed from the hotel, taking no notice of the confused and questioning looks he received from those of his fighters he passed, the giant in his wake. Adamenko realized that Orlov was headed for the theater. A sudden sickening feeling in the pit of his stomach told him that they had been duped. The attack was just a diversion and somehow...

They rushed into the deserted lobby. There was no sound from within the theater, and although the doorway to the auditorium was closed, there was a sense of emptiness that told them exactly what they would find when they entered.

Orlov cursed and kicked uselessly at a discarded chair as he took in a room empty except for the corpse of one of his men. Adamenko looked on, not knowing what to say to make it better for his friend, wondering how the Russians had managed to penetrate the town, and fighting the rising red mist of hatred and anger that threatened to overwhelm him. He knew that he had to try to keep control as Orlov would need him at his side, not going crazy until it was necessary.

So it was that, with the effort to assimilate all these things, the giant's voice came out so small and lost. It cut through Orlov's rage, and reminded him suddenly of those years when they were children and the hate and pride that had first bound them together. He stopped his raging, and was still.

"I tell you what we do. The only thing we can. We talk to this scum tank commander and find what it is that he wants."

"He has what he wants, Alexei. They are gone."

"Then why hasn't he reduced us to rubble yet?"

"Maybe he does not yet know that he has what he wants," Adamenko ventured.

Orlov smiled slowly. "Yes… And if he does not know, then they have not escaped us yet. Rally the men, make a search, Viktor. I will try to contact this tank commander, see what he wants and what he knows. We may yet be able to salvage this and turn it to our advantage."

Orlov turned on his heel and led Adamenko back through the now almost empty and deserted streets to the hotel, where his radio was still in the suite cluttered by the corpses of the mayor and his wife.

Orlov ignored them as he picked up his radio, directing Adamenko to retrieve the one he had left earlier in his own room. Having done that, he led the giant back down to the streets.

"Alexei, I don't—"

Orlov cut him off. "Simple. We are using these old radios because they do not use the same frequency bands as cell phones, and we wanted to not only control the incoming and outgoing messages by cutting the cell mast in and out, we also wished to avoid being overheard by cell scanners. Unless you have the exact frequency, or very old equipment like this to make a scan, it is almost impossible to eavesdrop on these. They are perfect because they are so old they fall outside current usable technology."

"But what has that to do with the tanks?" Adamenko asked, puzzled.

Orlov shook his head. "Russian tanks are still old-fashioned in some ways. They may have a more sophisticated setup than before, but it still works in a similar way. If we use our main transmitter to scan the available radio frequencies, we can find their communications and so talk to them."

Adamenko was about to ask if it may not be quicker and easier to walk out himself with a white flag and a message when his thoughts—and their progress—were interrupted by the approach of a rebel fighter.

"Blokhin? Why are you not in position?" Orlov asked as the man hurriedly neared them.

Blokhin shook his head. "No time. Something strange happening." He was breathless, and it took him several gulps of air before he was able to continue. "I have had people ask me about the number of our men who have been seen heading toward the old warehouses, and why they are leading a group of civilians."

Orlov was puzzled. He looked at Adamenko and could see that the giant was just as baffled. "How many of us?" he questioned, and when the breathless Blokhin held up six fingers, he continued. "That's ridiculous—half of our personnel. Did they recognize any of our men?"

Blokhin looked puzzled. "They didn't say. I didn't think to ask. Why?"

Orlov was about to speak, but seemingly changed his mind. Shaking his head, he said, "It doesn't matter. All you need to know is that these men have nothing to do with us. I want you to get on the radio and draw as many men as possible to that sector. Get them to leave the citizens organizing their own security."

"Who are they?" Blokhin queried.

"They must be Russians," Orlov explained briefly. "It doesn't matter who. All that matters is that we stop and contain them. We must not press them too hard, as we can't risk the Americans being hurt."

"The Americans? Then—"

Orlov interrupted. "The shelling was a cover for them to extract the Americans so that they can flatten the town. If we stop them leaving, then we stop an attack. Go now and deal with this while I speak with the tank commander."

The rebel could see how perilous the situation was, and

as he turned away his face was colored with fear, even as he stuck to his task. Orlov beckoned the giant to follow him and made his way into the building where he had taken over the mayor's old office, the central transmitter for the radio comm system being set up here.

The operator looked up at him, expectant, as he entered. There was something about his bearing now that suggested purpose. He asked the radio operator to open as many channels and broadcast across as wide a frequency band as possible before beginning.

"This is Aleksandr Orlov, Commander of the Chechen National Socialist Army. Identify the frequency on which you wish to speak, and I will switch to it. We must talk before any further action is taken...."

"You see, Daman? All good things come to those who wait," General Azhkov said with a smile as the message came over the comm system. "Is it me, or is that a man who sounds desperate?"

Tankian wasn't sure that he would entirely agree. The voice on the radio sounded urgent but not as panicked as he would have expected from a man who was about to face annihilation.

General Azhkov indicated to his radio operator to send the correct frequency and leave the channel open, which he did. He waited patiently until he heard the rebel leader announce himself once more. Then he beckoned to his operator, and took the handset himself.

"I am General Sergei Azhkov, and I have a load of hardware trained right on you and your town. I am not in the mood to waste words. I don't know what you expect from the Russian government, and to tell the truth, I don't care. But I will tell you what will happen. In the morning, I will be ordered to fire on you, and to keep firing, clearing a path for my command to advance and roll over Argun-Martan. As you retreat into the open, you will be picked off by fighter jets."

"So nice of you to tell me what our fate will be." Orlov's voice crackled evenly over the static. "There is just one thing that may stop you in this plan."

Azhkov gave Tankian a look that indicated his disbelief. "Believe me, my friend, there is nothing that can stop me. It is not down to me," he said with heavy emphasis. "This will happen. I showed you what it will be like in order for you to talk as I do not want to kill innocent townspeople—"

"No, you listen, Sergei Azhkov, and I, Alexsandr Orlov, will tell you how it is. You shell us to provide a diversion for your men to come into the town and take the Americans. But they are not with you, are they?"

"You foolish little man, what are you talking about?" Azhkov raged. "I am offering you a chance to head off your inevitable destruction, and all you can do is try to feed me some shit about my people taking the Americans... You idiot, I do not care about the Americans, and if you think the president does—"

"The president has spoken to me, and I have explained to him what it is that the Americans know, and what that is worth both to Russia and America, as well as to the Chechen people. He would not—"

"Shut up, you complete prick," Azhkov raged. Despite the constrictions of space within the tank, the general was on his feet, his arms waving wildly in frustration. "What part of what I have told you do you not grasp? The president does not care about the Americans. He will blame their deaths on you and be believed, as you have allowed a whole town to be flattened. I am offering you a chance to come to agreement and withdraw before I have to grind you to dust and leave the remains for trigger-happy pilots."

"The more you rage, the more you show your frustration at your plan not working," Orlov's voice crackled back. "We have your men cornered and the Americans will soon be back within our grasp. Once this is achieved, your plans will not matter. Tell your president that we will negotiate with him alone, and not with some middleman."

The radio went dead, with not even the crackle of empty air to indicate any presence.

"The prick has turned off his radio," Azhkov murmured in astonishment, staring at the radio transmitter and shaking his head in disbelief. "Is he in denial or is he just insane?"

"I don't know, Sergei," Tankian said. "What the hell was he talking about? Our men trying to take the Americans... What the hell does he mean?"

"I don't know," Azhkov replied in a voice that was flat and yet teetered on the edge of barely controlled menace. "He is either completely crazy, or there is something going on that we do not know about."

"Could the U.S. government have sent in a team to extract the Americans?"

Azhkov shook his head. "It is, I suppose, a possibility. But a remote one. How could anyone move in this area without us having some kind of indication? He is bluffing."

"Are you sure? I mean, why would he do that?"

Azhkov turned to face Tankian, and his slablike face was filled with a cold fury that made Tankian's blood run to ice.

"Because he is an opportunist. Because he thinks I am an idiot. Because he is deluded. I do not know, and frankly neither do I care. He takes me for an idiot, when it is him who is foolish. He had his chance. He's blown it. Now I will blow him off the face of the earth."

Snatching up the radio handset once more, General Azhkov yelled orders.

ORLOV CUT COMMUNICATIONS and turned to Adamenkov, his face black with fury. "Who does this prick think he is? Does he really think that we will believe him? Come, Viktor, the only way we are going to make him take us seriously is if we cut off the heads of the soldiers he has sent in, and send them back to him on poles. Then he will know that we are not to be messed with."

The giant grinned. At last he would have the chance to take out some of his frustration over the night's events. The idea of being able to kill and mutilate some Russians calmed him inside. He followed Orlov out onto the street, breathing slowly but heavily as he built himself up into the kind of rage he would need.

As the two rebels strode through the streets, they could see that the route toward the industrial area of town was devoid of their own men, as they were greeted by small groups of townspeople who were armed and patrolling their own streets. Orlov felt a warm glow at their greeting. This kind of cooperation between Chechens was exactly what he had been looking for all his life. The fact that his own men—an occupying force according to the hated Russians—could leave the town unguarded and the citizens would step into the breach only showed how out of touch the fool Russian president was with the people of Chechnya. When this matter had been resolved, and he was able to grow from Argun-Martan the seeds of a genuine revolution, then he would show that idiot Russian what the Chechen people could achieve.

He was still fuming, and lost in these thoughts, as he

and Adamenko approached the deserted industrial area of town. Not, perhaps, so deserted: there was the intermittent chatter of automatic rifle fire. It was sporadic, and to anyone versed in combat spoke of a cagey exchange between an attacking force and one that had dug itself in well.

"We have them pinned down," Orlov said to his companion, but could see from the faraway look in the giant's eyes that he was already focused on attack. This, then, should not take long.

As they came in sight of their men, they could see that they had spread around the perimeter of a disused factory unit. They had the Americans and the Russians who had taken them trapped. Now it was just a matter of smoking them out—literally. Orlov directed the giant to get a gas mask and an SMG, and told his men to lay down covering fire after firing gas and smoke grenades into the building. Adamenko was his blunt force attack weapon, and this was the perfect time to use him.

It was a simple plan, and would have been effective if not for one thing: as his men moved to fire the grenades, and before the first one had even left its launcher, the night sky howled with the sound of a barrage of shells cutting through the air. Moments later that was followed by a series of explosions that rent the air around them and made the ground shake violently. Darkness turned to light as a rain of fire began to sweep the far end of town, the flames lighting the factory and grounds in front of them.

Orlov realized that Azhkov had not believed him for one reason alone: whoever was in there had nothing to do with the Russians. But it was far too late to worry about that now.

17

Bolan had realized that things were going wrong from the moment that they started to see people on the streets again. Despite the men on point, it was hard to keep a tight hold on the group as some of them were flagging under the physical and mental pressure of trying to escape. The pace that Bolan had set was hard—it had to be—and yet it was proving to be just that little too much for some. As a result, they had started to string out along the streets rather than keep together, and even though the point men had managed to scout a clear path, those at the rear had attracted attention.

The locals who came out were waved back, imprecations in Chechen assuring them that all was well and that they should stay inside as directed. That may have been enough. Bolan was all too aware that any one of them could raise an alarm, ask enough of a question to bring the rebels down on them. There didn't seem a large force in the town, and maybe his men could take them. But maybe was not enough when he had the survey team to protect and evacuate. They needed to move fast.

As they reached the deserted factories and industrial warehouses that populated the outer reaches of the town, Bolan became aware that they were being shadowed. Ahead and alongside them, in and out of the darkness, he could see that rebel fighters were moving in on them, getting ahead where they were faster and more mobile. That was a problem. Word passed between his men showed that they were also aware, and that the two point men were concerned they could not guarantee safe passage. Bolan checked his watch. Time was tight enough as it was; they couldn't afford to be held up any more.

He wasn't going to have any choice in the matter. The crackle of gunfire in the silence of the night, the whine of brickwork chips as the bullets flew high and wide and the muted squeals and shouts of the survey team told him that they would have to find a place to stand and fight. And, if they got through this, hope that Jack Grimaldi could hang around for them if the numbers counted down to zero.

An answering chatter of gunfire from Krilov and Dostoyevsky stopped the enemy bullets for a moment. There was a factory building a few hundred yards from where they stood: the gates were broken, and beyond Bolan could see—even in the dark—that the entrance had long been left open and exposed. Once inside he could put a man on it. The key was to get the civilians under cover and then work on picking off the opposition. To lure them to his men was just about his only option right now.

Yelling at the survey team to move, Bolan directed the group toward the grounds of the factory. Looking around, even with infrared night vision it would have been almost impossible to pick out the rebel fighters as they used the cover of the surrounding buildings with the kind of skill he would have expected from their knowledge of the area. Once inside it would be a different matter.

Although he only had six men, the Executioner knew that there were no more than a dozen of the rebels out there. If they wanted to get the survey team back, they could play the long game or be forced to mount a full-on attack across ground that would leave them exposed as they came. Bolan knew that the presence of the Russian tanks would force their hand.

It was hard to get the survey team across the grounds of the factory in any kind of order. The sporadic fire that kicked up divots all around them caused some of them to panic and try to run. It was Bulgarin who proved his worth by shepherding them into the entrance. Bolan got his men to take the former hostages to the upper level of the building, with Krilov marshaling them onto the top floor while the other mercenaries took defensive positions along the way. The men who had taken point were the last to enter, and Bolan stayed on the ground floor to see them safely in before sending them up to the top. They and Bulgarin would take up defensive positions near the barred and boarded windows, visible glass smashed out so that they could sight the enemy from all four compass points. It was only when the posts had been established that Bolan joined the men on the top floor.

The appearance of the gas-masked giant, striding across the open ground and ignoring the shots that kicked up dirt around him alerted Bolan to the coming attack. The sounds of firing and the shattering of glass and boards as the gas and smoke grenades hit home made him curse. He had gambled that they wouldn't do this, fearing for the prize they valued so highly.

As Bolan and his mercenaries scrambled into their gas masks, he realized that something had happened to change this rebel view. The thought was reinforced as the night erupted around them.

As the choking clouds of smoke and gas started to fill the upper floor, thankfully dissipated enough for the survey team to breathe a little by the crosswinds seeping through the shattered windows, he was aware of the chatter of fire from below and a bellow of rage that greeted the volley.

The giant was inside.

The survey team was in disarray. It was Leonard's job to keep the Americans together. His purpose: to get his people away and try to keep them safe. He was to leave the fighting to the men who were skilled and in combat. If he could keep his people together, then it would allow the others to concentrate on the attack.

They weren't going to make it easy. The sudden noise and fury of the tank attack combined with the incoming grenades had hit Simmons like a sledgehammer, rousing him from his cocoon so that he suddenly rose to his feet, shouting and blindly attempting to flee. Slaughter and Winters tried to hold him back, but they were taken off guard. Shouting and crying, Simmons cannoned into Acquero, pushing her back so that she stumbled blindly toward the window manned by Bolan.

The survey team had been marshaled into the middle of the floor to keep them as much away from the line of fire as was possible: Simmons was almost singlehandedly trying to blow this plan out of the water. He dragged Slaughter and Winters out of the center, pushed Acquero back and then tried to change direction, causing Freeman to also break rank as he dived across the floor and grabbed Simmons around the waist, tackling him as if he was a quarterback and bringing him down to the floor. The impact was enough to knock the wind out of Simmons, quieting him.

Damage was already done. Acquero stumbled backward across the floor, catching Bolan and knocking him so that he fired wide of the clustered rebels below. That wasn't a problem; the fact that the move brought her in line with the open space and the gunfire that was directed at

it was, however, a real problem. As random fire spattered
the walls around and inside the factory, Acquero was a
flailing target.

Bolan grabbed her and pulled her to the floor. She
gasped, and for a second he thought that she was hit. It
was only when she tried to wriggle free that he realized
the gasp had been from the impact of the fall alone. With
a grin, he pushed himself up and allowed her to scrabble
back to the center of the room, where Freeman was help-
ing Leonard to keep the group together, aided by those
who were keeping their cool under trying circumstances.

Bolan was relieved to leave them to their own provenance, as there were greater problems immediately in
front of him.

He could hear the roar of the giant down one floor along
with the screams of at least one of his men, shouts of pain
and terror intermingled with the giant's bellowing.

"Cover this," Bolan yelled at Leonard, indicating the
window he had been attending. "Quick!"

The security man glanced at the survey team. Freeman gave him a nod. The young engineer was proving his
worth, directing the others to keep the more vulnerable
members of the group contained. Acquero, too, nodded
and gave him a smile.

Damn, Leonard was glad those two were around, he
thought as he moved to take over from the big American.
He sighted on the rebels below, sending out covering fire
to try to keep them from moving forward or firing any
more gas or smoke grenades. As he did this, he allowed
the soldier to back up his men below.

Bolan headed for the stairwell. The top floor of the factory had been lit up by the fire that swept through the town,
and that only served to emphasize the darkness into which
he was descending. He lost the gas mask as the cooler in-

terior air became clearer, and flipped the night-vision goggles over his eyes. Immediately the stairwell became…

Clearer? Maybe in vision, but not in making sense of what he was seeing. One man lay half-hidden by a wall separating the factory floor from the stairwell. A pool of blood had spread out around him, and a severed hand lay to one side of him. His legs were bent at an unnatural angle that suggested every bone in them had been broken.

Had the giant been able to do that? Why hadn't he been fired on by the guards Bolan had stationed?

Maybe what was happening just out of sight would provide an answer. Even above the chatter of gunfire and roar of shellfire from beyond, within the thick walls of the factory it was still possible to hear the sounds of hand-to-hand combat.

Bolan moved cautiously down the remaining steps until he was standing on the factory floor, shielded by the wall. He looked down at the dead man at his feet. The face and head had been battered so severely that in this light—even with the night-vision goggles—it was impossible to work out who it was.

The Executioner brought up his SMG so that it nestled in his shoulder, braced himself and then slowly moved around the wall so that he had the whole floor in view.

The sight that greeted him made him pause. Bolan had seen a lot of things over the years, but very rarely had there been anything to make him stop and stare.

This came close. He could see now why his men had not been able to fire on the giant: there were two rifles across the floor, broken from the impact they had made on the bricks of the factory walls, chunks of which lay around them. A discarded SMG and a gas mask spoke of the giant's determination to be—quite literally—hands-on in his attack. For in the middle of the floor, two men whirled in a circle, Bolan's man clinging to the giant if only because he had the larger man's arms pinned, and so could prevent the giant inflicting more pain on him.

He wouldn't be able to hang on much longer. The giant was repeatedly head-butting him as they swung around, and the soldier could see blood spraying from his man's head with each blow. Finally it was one blow too many, and the merc let go, stunned almost to the point of insensibility. He staggered back, reeling and coming to rest on his knees, facing the giant rebel fighter, who stood impassive over him.

At least Bolan was now able to get a clear sight of the giant. The man was wearing heavy Kevlar, which was why much of the fire directed at him had failed to kill him. The ripped camou clothing showed it beneath, the continuous fire having taken its toll on a vest that was almost hanging from him. Even so, the impact alone should have been enough to stop him. And he had been hit in several places, flesh wounds bleeding heavily from his limbs. He should be down.

What was keeping him upright? Drugs? Adrenaline? As Bolan got a clear look at his face, he could see that it was blank, the giant's eyes wired and wild. The rebel was in some kind of self-induced hypnotic state that drove him on regardless. As Bolan watched, the giant pulled a short-handled ax from inside his dangling Kevlar and raised it, dragging breath and bringing forth a mighty cry that rang around the echoing, empty room.

The mercenaries had tried to take him out with body shots, and had failed because of his immense strength and his armor. One of them was already dead; the other one was about to die after a beating that was tactically unnecessary, but had to have somehow fuelled and fed the giant's rage.

The mercenaries had made mistakes because they had tackled him like any regular fighter. They hadn't had time to adjust before he had been on top of them.

Bolan had that luxury, and although his teammate looked dead already, he also had the opportunity to save him. The soldier sighted for the center of the giant's head, set his weapon to continuous fire and squeezed.

A deafening volley of gunfire filled the almost-empty factory floor. The giant's head split like an overripe melon as Bolan followed his stumbling gait, caught off balance by the SMG burst. Even the force of the impact gave the giant no escape as Bolan adjusted aim, pouring fire on him as he fell. The ax clattered from his nerveless hand onto the concrete floor, and Bolan moved swiftly into the room, ceasing fire as the giant twitched, his head barely recognizable.

Barely identifiable through the blood and swelling of his face, Dostoyevsky raised himself slowly and tried to grin as Bolan came to his side. "Thanks, Cooper. I don't think he was going to kill me quick. Maybe you should. I'm no use to you now."

"We don't leave our own behind, not while they're alive," Bolan said firmly, eyeing Vishniev's mangled body. But even as he did, he was checking Dostoyevsky. As much as he meant what he said, he realized that it would be difficult. The mercenary was unable to sit upright, and as he listed he winced with pain as his shattered elbow and shoulder took weight. One ankle looked twisted at an unnatural angle. He was bleeding from several places, his clothing darkened in patches that were spreading.

"You're not getting me up there," the mercenary said with a grimace. "Leave me here—give me that gun," he added, offering his good hand. "Prop me up and pick me up when you go. I'll keep us covered. Your plan?"

Bolan grinned; the Russian had guts. "Your countrymen are attacking the town. If we can keep the rebels at bay until they're called back, or even take them down, then the confusion should allow us to get out and get to the rendezvous point. Most forces will be concentrated on holding back the tanks."

"I would have thought so. They're fast bastards," the Russian said with grim humor.

Bolan realized what he meant. "Not so fast that we can't carry you. There are enough of us."

"Then I suggest you get back up there and leave me to take sentry," the Russian said, wheezing with the effort of propping himself upright.

Bolan nodded and left Dostoyevsky where he lay; looking back at the mercenary as he doggedly set his sights, he wondered if the man had enough strength to make it out.

There was only one way to find out. First, though, he had to clear a path for the survey team to get them extracted successfully.

Running back up the stairs, he could hear that the firing from the top floor had ceased. When he reached the top, he came up short. What greeted him explained why there was no firing, but presented him with a major problem.

Bulgarin and Krilov were facing off from opposite sides of the floor, guns directed at each other rather than the enemy. The survey team was huddled in the middle of the floor, with Leonard standing over the top of them, his own rifle trained on the Russian. Basayev stood apart, his weapon still trained on the action outside.

"Hey, Cooper, good thing you've come back," he yelled. "Try and calm that Russian bastard, will you?"

18

Vassilev groaned as he pulled himself to his feet. He still felt groggy, and his head was pounding like a jackhammer. He tried to remember what he had been doing, and where the hell he was. As he picked himself up and dusted himself down, he looked around. He was in a building that was derelict. Recently, by the look of it: the dust was still settling, and the timbers hanging from the caved-in ceiling creaked ominously. Outside, he could hear people rushing, panicking, and the noises of fire.

He experienced a jumble of images and sensations, but eventually he pieced it together. He had entered the deserted shop as it was perfect for a recce position. He had headed to the upper story to get a good view of the rebels' emplacements, and with the binoculars he'd be able to see the tank regiment beyond.

And then the Russians had fired. Although the shop had not been hit directly, shrapnel from the shell had taken out the roof of the building, causing the cave-in. Although his entire body ached, Vassilev could tell that he had been incredibly lucky and that nothing was broken. Maybe he had a bit of a concussion, but nothing that he couldn't sleep off later. He was alive, and that was all that mattered. The only problem was that he was, in combat terms, useless now. His weapons were gone, buried and lost under the rubble, as was his radio. He searched for it near to where he had lain, and found what was left of it.

He cursed and looked at his watch. By some miracle, it was still working. Little time remained until the rendezvous. Maybe, if he was lucky, he could still make that.

The sudden eruption of the night into a shower of shells and a storm of fire suggested that luck may not be on his side. Cursing louder, the Georgian figured his best move was to get out of the building before it finally crashed down all around him.

Outside on the street, he passed for a rebel as his clothing was mostly intact, the blacksuit hardly showing. In the confusion that sprung up, this was enough. The streets became full of citizens, some panicking and others flocking to the front line to help defend the town. He dodged between the groups and clusters of people, hardly noticed as he sought to find a path through the carnage and maybe pick up a weapon.

His progress was delayed by collapsing buildings and the flash and deafening blasts of shells. The fires they caused blocked streets and alleys, forcing him to double back. The move was not without one advantage, as he stumbled over the corpse of a rebel fighter, his AK-47 intact even though half of his torso was missing.

Providence would always provide, the mercenary figured, picking up the rifle and stripping the corpse of its spare ammunition. The only thing providence was not doing was giving him a clear route to safety. If anything, it was driving him back toward the front line.

It was then that he saw Orlov. The rebel leader was running through the streets, looking terrified. Vassilev recognized him from their briefing. A man that terrified would most likely have an escape route mapped out, the Georgian figured. Maybe he was worth following.

Figuring once more that providence would provide, Vassilev set off in pursuit.

"COOPER, IT'S SIMPLE. These idiots have found something that is of great worth to my people. It should go to them, not to the United States. The move on Argun-Martan should not have happened until daylight, but that does not affect the plan. We move them out of town, then we are picked up by a detachment from the air force that will be sent for us."

"If it belongs to anyone, it belongs to my people," Krilov growled. "You will not take it from them."

"Listen," Basayev interrupted, "you're like me—you're only Chechen when there's no cash involved. We get paid for taking these people back to the Americans. Screw this Russian freak. Kill him and let's move."

Bulgarin smiled. "He cannot kill me. He knows I would drop him first."

"So what if I do it? You can't take us both out," Bolan said, although his demeanor did not reflect his tone. He seemed relaxed, uncaring. In the center of the floor, the survey team was cowering. Leonard gave Bolan a puzzled stare but did not speak, waiting to see what the soldier would do.

"Yours was an arranged op, with no opportunity of contact once you had infiltrated us. How long have you been playing this game? Freelance but undercover?"

"So long I can't remember which I was first, but not so long that I don't know who pays me more. Or where I'm from. The timescale is screwed, but as long as I get these people to the right point—"

"And how are you going to take all of us down?" Bolan asked.

Bulgarin laughed. "Three are gone already—I'm guessing that the big one took out the guards, and Vassilev is long gone. That leaves you three, and maybe the big black guy," he added, indicating Leonard. "The idea was to take you out as we left for the rendezvous, one by one. It's not going to work that way, so it's death or glory." He lowered his SMG so that it was leveled now at the survey team. "You fire on me, I spray 'n pray as I go. Not much point you going home with body bags, is there?"

They were at an impasse. Whatever his original plan had been, the Russian now had a simple strategy. If he could not take the survey team, then no one could. He was banking on Bolan's desire to achieve his mission objective. With his SMG trained on the group, and with Argun-Martan about to be reduced to ashes and rubble, Bolan was running out of options.

"Kill them," he said. "Do it. Then I kill you. You really think you can get them out of here and to your rendezvous point without having to kill us? And what about when they scatter outside? Because they will. The bombing or their own fear will do that. Which ones are the most valuable? Which ones do you kill as an example and which ones do you save?"

Although his voice was calm and steady, the soldier's pulse raced and he could feel sweat bead on his forehead. He was aware of the shelling outside as it pounded the town. He was aware of the fact that it was getting closer as the tanks began to advance. He was aware of the firestorm it had caused, and how the night breeze was sweeping the flames toward them. There was no barrage from outside now, as the rebels had either been withdrawn to defend the front line, or had just scattered of their own volition. If they could get out of the factory quickly, they would probably have a clear path to the rendezvous point.

As he spoke, Bolan was aware that Leonard and one of the survey team, a young black guy, had been exchanging glances and discreet hand signals. From his position in the group, the young man was slowly moving so that he crossed those who were in the direct line of fire. Leonard moved slowly, too, coming forward. He could see Bolan looking at him, and their eyes met for a moment.

Bolan could see that the young man was willing to act as a human shield, and that the security man was also prepared to throw himself into the line of fire.

He couldn't allow such sacrifice. He threw down his weapons and stepped toward the center of the floor.

"Okay, you win," he said, holding up his hands. "We do it your way."

Bulgarin grinned mirthlessly and turned his SMG on Bolan. "I knew you'd see it my way," he muttered, squeezing the trigger.

The Executioner threw himself sideways, feeling the burst of rounds catch at his shoulder and upper arm. He moved downward, and the burst was deflected up by the sudden jerk of the gunman. It was enough to save his life, but not his entire skin as the burning pain made him wince and grunt through gritted teeth.

It had been enough, though. He had hoped that Leonard would somehow read his intent and if not he had at least been quick enough to pick up the thread. In attempting to eliminate the soldier quickly, Bulgarin's attention had been shifted just long enough for Leonard to fire a burst that sent the Russian staggering toward the open window. Taking their cue, Basayev and Krilov had also fired on him, the force of the combined fire sending the Russian through the open space and down to the ground floor.

The room was filled with the smell of cordite and the echo of the chattering cross fire as it slowly died away.

Acquero and Leonard were at Bolan's side, already tending to his wounds. Basayev and Krilov joined them.

"It's clear out there, boss. If we're going to get going... You up to it?"

Bolan grinned. "It's not my legs, I'll be fine. I might only be able to hold a gun one-handed, though. Listen— Dostoyevsky is still alive, but you'll need a stretcher of some kind. I figure these two and that young black guy can shepherd the hostages. They've got the guts. Give them some ordnance, and you take Dostoyevsky. If we're still breathing, we all go."

Basayev shook his head. "You're mad, boss. I thought you were dead meat."

"Not yet," Bolan replied. "Not if I have any say."

VASSILEV FOLLOWED ORLOV through the streets, past men and women who were now in flight as the destruction spread, hardly noticing the two men who were pushing against the flow. The streets were bleeding into each other as the fires spread and the buildings crumbled under the onslaught. The Georgian was baffled by the behavior of the rebel leader. Where was he going, and what was he hoping to achieve? The town was falling around him, and there was no way that he was going to stop the tank onslaught. If he had any sense, he would try to fall back, regroup, gather as many of his men as he could muster.

But no, it was as though the rebel leader felt that he had a personal date with destiny.

Part of the Georgian wanted to take him down and then try to make his way out of this inferno and head for the rendezvous. Maybe he would be the only one. Maybe he would be able to link up with the others if they had made it through this. Whatever, he would have to move if he was to do it.

Part of Vassilev, though, was curious as to what the rebel leader was doing, and what he hoped to achieve. It was almost a compulsion to follow and see.

They neared the edge of town. The exact line of delineation had disappeared, swept away by the bombardment. The post where the rebel leader had first observed the tanks was lost, and Vassilev watched as Orlov passed the point without even realizing it was there. He was walking over rubble, ignoring the fires that raged around him and the shells that flew over his head and into the town that lay to his rear.

Orlov stood alone and unarmed on a pile of rubble, holding up his arms. In supplication? In surrender? Or as a command to stop?

If it was the latter, Vassilev was astounded to see it work. The leading tank rumbled to a halt a bare ten meters from the lone rebel. The others flanking it slowed and came to a halt. For a moment the bombardment ceased, and the incessant pounding of the shelling was silenced, allowing only for the sounds of the burning town and the shattered populace to filter through.

The turret of the lead tank opened and a man with a cold, hard face like a slab of frozen meat appeared. His face split in a malicious grin, and he raised a microphone to his lips, the sound coming from a loudspeaker hidden in the body of the vehicle.

"Little man, are you Aleksandr Orlov?"

"I am," Orlov yelled back. "I command you to stop. This is an independent state, and we have valuable resources, the destruction of which will bring down on you and your government international opprobrium."

"Words. Words, you stupid little man. I am General Sergei Azhkov, and I will be alive to explain myself while you are dead. What use are all your resources to you then?"

"History will judge me," Orlov yelled, a sob in his voice.

"History will forget you. And what will you care? You won't be here," Azhkov said with a shrug, disappearing back down into his tank with a terrible finality.

Vassilev realized that the rebel leader had no plan, only madness. The confrontation would write his death warrant, and the Georgian had no intention of being around to get caught up in the proceedings. He turned and headed back into town, picking up the pace in anticipation of what would happen next.

It was inevitable. The bombardment started again with an unannounced suddenness that mirrored its temporary cessation. The Georgian scrambled over ruins, and back into streets that were lit by flame, the walls of once secure and safe dwellings falling around him. The town was deserted now, the people either dead under the rubble or pulled back to those parts where the shells had not yet reached, perhaps—hopefully—on their way to the road that led out of the town and into the safety of the hills. He didn't blame them, but hoped to God that their flight would not interfere with his own passage to the rendezvous point.

He did not see Orlov stand firm on his small platform of rubble, arms aloft, trying to hold back the tide of history as it swept over him, the general ordering his tank to plow straight ahead, regardless of whatever lay in its path. Even if some of what lay in that path was human and alive.

The tank track plowed the rebel leader into the rubble that lay beneath him. His cries and screams—as much of frustration as of pain—were lost in the sounds of the tank engine and the crunching of debris. His presence did not register as so much as a bump to those who sat within the tank. They did not notice as they passed; the rebels were unimportant. All that mattered now was finishing the job they had started.

And Vassilev was not the only one who needed to get out before they had achieved that aim.

BOLAN TOOK POINT as the group left the factory.

Basayev and Krilov carried Dostoyevsky, while Freeman took the dead Bulgarin's SMG, and after a crash course from Leonard accompanied the older security man as the guard for the survey team.

Ironically, despite the fact that they were carrying wounded and were down on combat experience, they found it easy to negotiate the streets and alleys that took them out of Argun-Martan and into the area leading toward the lower hills of the Caucasus. They were not alone. They appeared to be joining an exodus from the town as the survivors who were able to move swiftly rushed past them, their possessions on their backs or loaded into carts as the streets were impassable for cars. The mercenaries were still in rebel dress, but they and the Americans were ignored, apart from a few muttered oaths and curses directed at them in the misplaced belief they were part of the National Socialists.

It was a complete capitulation. As Bolan and the others left the town behind them and trekked across the flat plain to the foothills, they could hear the town's buildings collapsing, the roar of fire, shell detonation and falling masonry a constant backdrop. They were accompanied part of the way by some of the townspeople, and even a couple of rebel fighters, who did not give them a second glance as an enmity had ended with the destruction of the town.

As they reached the foothills, and the sun started to rise, the crowds thinned out as the townspeople dispersed to farmsteads where their family and friends would take them in until the battle died down.

Bolan took in the sunrise and checked his watch. They were well past the rendezvous time, and he would have been surprised if Jack Grimaldi had hung around. There would be a Russian air force presence in the region, and it wouldn't be politic for *Dragonslayer* to be caught in flight.

"We've missed him, right?" Basayev said, seeing Bolan's expression.

The soldier nodded. "It's okay. We had a contingency plan. If all else fails we make camp, and Jack tries again on the twenty-four-hour mark."

The Chechen eyed the skies. "Maybe a good idea, maybe not. We can hide okay, I guess, but I'm not sure…." He trailed off and looked down at Dostoyevsky, who was only semiconscious on the improvised stretcher.

Bolan nodded grimly. "We'll just have to hope."

"Maybe not," Krilov commented, his face rapt in concentration. "Listen…"

The sound of a chopper was cutting through the background noise, and before Bolan had a chance to answer the Chechen mercenary, Grimaldi piloted his craft through a narrow channel in the hills, skirting so low that the backwash of his blades almost cut them down as he approached.

The chopper swept over them, lowering its fuselage as far as possible. A nylon rope ladder whipped in the crosswinds of the downdraft. Leonard grabbed it and held it steady, indicating to Basayev and Krilov that one of them should go first. After an exchange of glances, Krilov scaled the ladder, leaving Basayev with Dostoyevsky.

"I like your pilot, boss, he's as crazy as you," the Chechen yelled at Bolan over the noise of the engines. "Listen, I'll stay down and go last when you've got him up there," he added, gesturing to the prone fighter.

Leonard came across to them. "You go after my people," he said to Bolan. "I've told Freeman to get them in order. I'll help with this guy." He gestured to Dostoyevsky. "Your shoulder won't let you be of any use right now."

Bolan nodded curtly. Meanwhile, the Chechen in the chopper had lowered a harness, which enabled the survey team to ascend quickly, one-by-one. Bolan went after Freeman, when the young man had gotten his people aboard. By the time that Leonard and Basayev had gotten the wounded mercenary aboard and were coming up themselves, Bolan was in the cockpit with Grimaldi.

"You had me worried there, Sarge," the Stony Man pilot said in a laconic tone that said otherwise. "Few scratches on the way back, I see."

"You surprised me— I was ready to settle everyone in for the day. Occupational hazard," he added, indicating the wound.

"I was here at the time," Grimaldi told him. "You weren't, and I did head back. But it looked a little heated in the town, so I cut you some slack. You were lucky— it was my last pass. I stripped her bare as possible, too. I figured we'd be carrying just over a full load."

"Should have been," Bolan said with a tinge of regret. "The hostages must have lost one before we arrived, I guess. No time to ask. And we lost two, with one MIA."

"Those are good odds considering what's going down." Grimaldi shrugged as he turned *Dragonslayer* and headed for the border.

"I guess so," Bolan affirmed, although it hurt that there would be one family who would not be welcoming their boy home.

CNN ANNOUNCED LATER that day that a U.S.-endorsed mission by the Russian army had resulted in the rebel Chechen forces being routed and a party of civilian American mining personnel being rescued and returned safely to the U.S. Embassy in Moscow. This operation had been planned between the two countries as a gesture of friendship after U.S. mining interests had reported finding vast new mineral reserves around the town of Argun-Martan, and had unfortunately found themselves innocently caught up in a nationalist uprising.

The U.S. government, the U.S. mining industry and the Russian government had worked together in cooperation to seal the financial union the corporations had formed with the Russian ministry, personally overseen by the Russian president, to forge a deal for co-development of the sites.

Two days later, the same channel reported on the arrival home of the rescued mining party, although no reporter thought to ask why they had flown in from Georgia rather than Moscow.

There was a man in a bar in Tblisi who knew why.

Vassilev raised a glass to them, glad that he had been able to hike to the border after seeing the chopper recede into the distance and wondering if he still had Cooper's contact number so that he could get his money.

* * * * *

AleX Archer
TREASURE OF LIMA

**A myth of the past holds the
promise of wealth…and death.**

Costa Rica's white beaches and coral reefs should have been
adventure-proof. But naturally, archaeologist and TV show
host Annja Creed's peace is
interrupted by a mysterious
woman with a strange tale.
Her husband has disappeared
after leading an expedition in
search of the "Lost Loot of
Lima." The treasure was lost
in the late nineteenth century,
when a Peruvian ship captain
had gone mad with greed. Now
Annja has been asked to lead a
fateful sojourn for the lost loot.
But where treasures are lost,
danger will always be found….

*Available January wherever
books and ebooks are sold.*

BH